Prince Avalask

- Halie Fewkes -

To Kaleb,

If you are new to the Secrets of The Tally Series, Welcome!

But don't start the series here!

You'll want to start with Book One – Secrets of The Tally.

Prince Avalask may be the prequel, but it shouldn't be read until you've at least finished Book Four.

This Prequel won't slow down to explain the core concepts – like what Escalis or Epics are – and it will also spoil *just about everything* in the first four books of the series. Don't do that to yourself – go pick up "Secrets of The Tally" and get started!

And to everybody who's caught up – Welcome to the prequel!

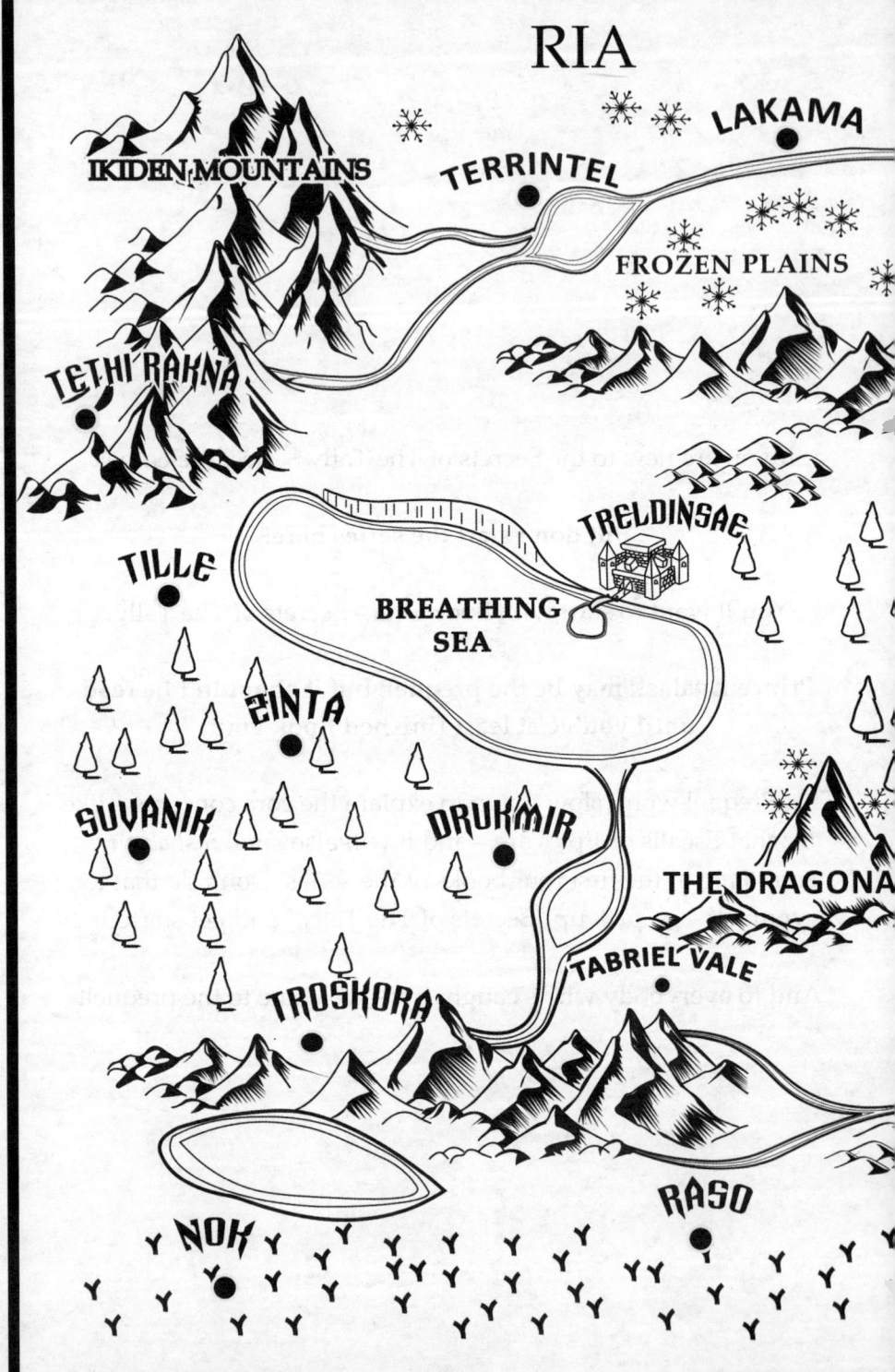

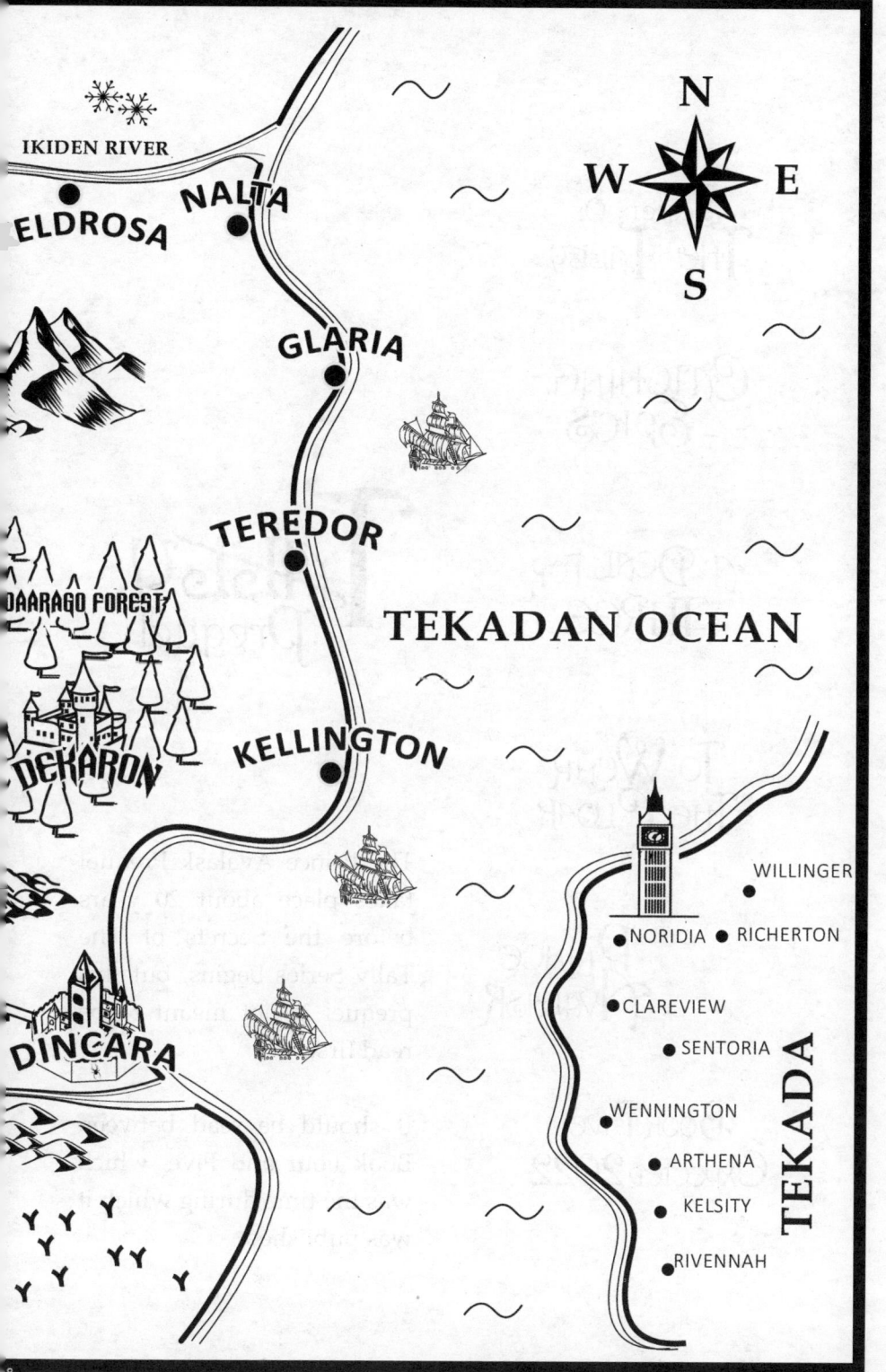

Secrets Of
The Tally

Catching
Epics

A Deal For
Three

To Wear
The Cloak

Prince
Avalask

Book Five
Expected 2022

Tally
Prequel

The Prince Avalask Prequel takes place about 20 years before the Secrets of The Tally Series begins, but this prequel is not meant to be read first.

It should be read between Book Four and Five, which was the time during which it was published.

THE ESCALI ROYAL FAMILY

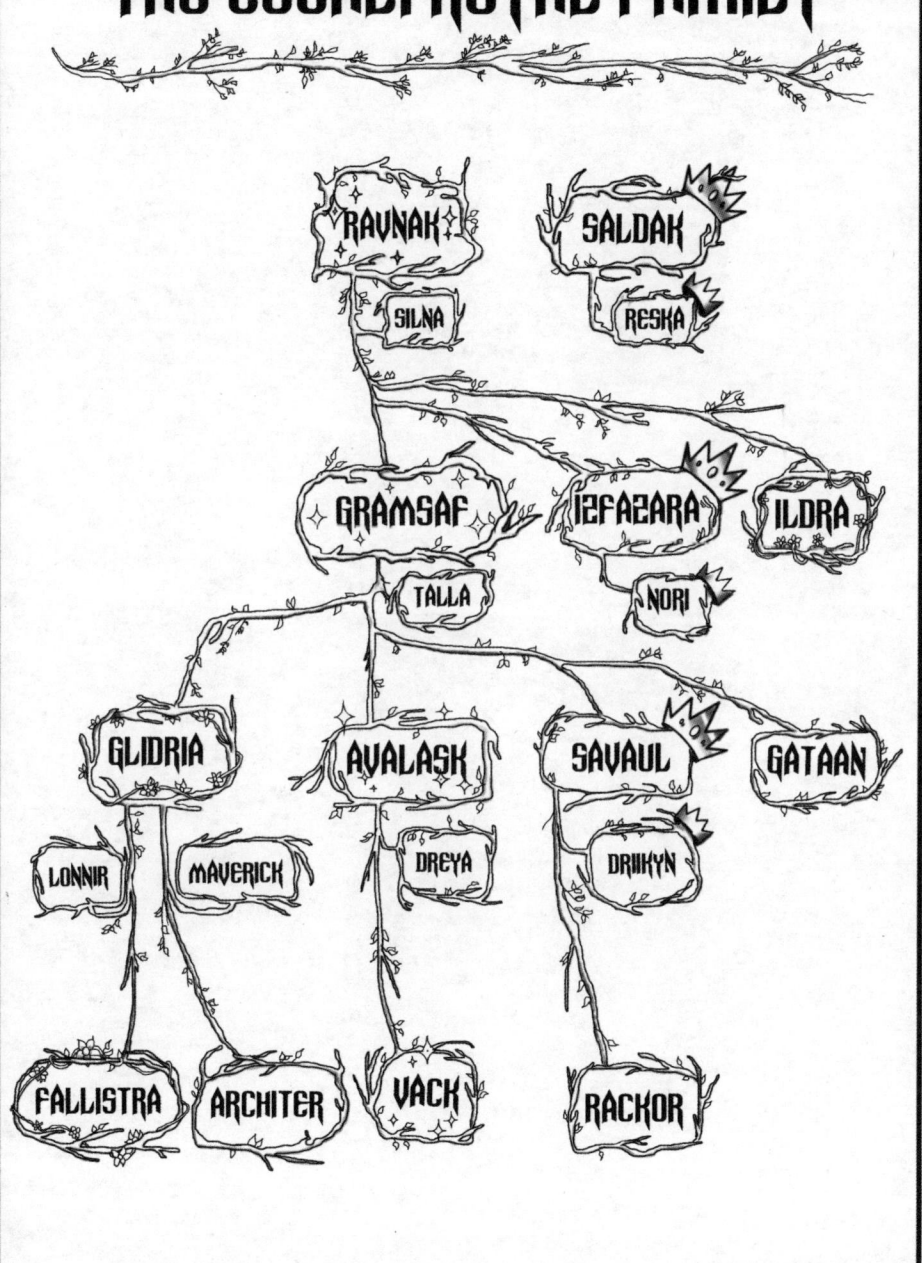

MAVERICK

PROLOGUE

Maverick's polished brown boots broke through a thin crust of snow with every step, and he took a deep breath of freezing air before he released it in a great cloud of fog. His black and grey snow-dog, Catch, knew he was having a moment of overwhelm, and stayed calmly at his side as Maverick rubbed his temple.

He'd come *so far* in mastering his powers since they'd first hit him in his pre-teen years. The ability to sense intentions was supposed to be a good, helpful power, but it had crippled him and nearly driven him insane when his gift came to him with an intensity he was sure nobody had ever survived before.

One day, he was a motivated farm boy with dreams bigger than the sky and no hope of ever seeing them fulfilled. The next, he began to realize he could sense the intentions of people around him and that every single living thing lived with intent and purpose — every person, every animal, every bit of flora, and every worm in the dirt. It started as an exciting revelation, but quickly turned into a curse as the sensitivity became excruciating. The intentions became a tsunami washing over him every second, drowning out every other sense. He couldn't shut them off.

Being in the room with even a single person had turned into a head-spinning nightmare as his powers manifested. Everyone was just a different tangle of self-preservation and self-gain, mixed with curiosity and the intent to learn, and usually the desire to extort

1

something of value from literally everything around them.

The intensity of it should have broken him — it *would* have destroyed anyone with a weaker soul or dimmer dreams. But Maverick had enough tenacity, even at the age of twelve, to see that if he could conquer the power instead of being conquered, maybe all his unbelievable ambitions would have ground to stand on.

And so he'd chosen to take control and persevere. He'd forced himself into silent meditation every day as he learned to take it all in, process the tidal wave of information trying to sweep him into its drowning depths, and somehow function at the same time.

And it took the next *seven years* to find any semblance of normal again.

Even now, at nineteen, he still resented venturing into the city where the cacophony clamored in his head until he felt sick. Tens of thousands of people, all with different goals, different purposes, different intents — just the notion of it all made him dizzy.

But he always made himself go. The overwhelm was just a weakness, and he was going to overcome it if he had to walk nauseously through Keldrosa every day for the rest of his life.

Maverick finally reached his destination — a small hideout tucked into a crevice between the mountain rocks, high in the hills away from the city. He took one last look at the forest of evergreens sparkling with frost, and then he pushed the thick white furs aside and climbed inside. This was his little oasis from the world — a place of respite where he could press his hands to his skull and regroup.

He'd been browsing through daggers in the market when the overwhelm had finally beaten him. The merchant selling the blades certainly thought he was on the verge of making a sale before Maverick had to curl his fingers over his temple and grit his teeth against the torment of the city's intentions reverberating through his head.

2

That poor salesman had no idea what to make of the sudden excuse to leave, and certainly would have never guessed that Maverick barely carried enough money for his next meal anyway. Nobody in town knew he was poor — they all thought he had money and status.

It was the way he carried himself, the clothes he wore, and his obsession with never allowing a stain or a wrinkle to tarnish his image. He spoke with a studied vocabulary and never let his expressions betray emotion, so when people looked at him, he appeared wise and wealthy. People were extremely accommodating when they thought that pleasing him would benefit them in some way. And he took advantage of that wherever he could.

He wasn't sure why Keldrosa had defeated him today — it had been weeks since he'd lost his grip on reality. Maybe it was the coming harvest, and everybody's feelings of purpose as the food they'd worked so hard to grow was finally ready to be plucked and stored. There was a scramble to get it all done before the freezing wind from the higher hills made its way into the valleys, and the city organizers were already hard at work planning the harvest festival for the end of the season. Maybe that was it. The intent of the city had just suddenly become too much.

The forest had calmer, gentler wants. The plants simply meant to survive, grow, and once a season, shed their leaves in preparation for winter — although not many deciduous trees happened to grow in the rocky elevations of his hideout.

Animals were more complicated, with real intents that matched a Human's — just in a more limited range. Maverick could feel a few small thoughts around him — probably winter mice working on a seed-harvest of their own. Catch lay next to him with the intent to support and please at the top of his mind. Thank life for dogs — they were infinitely more loyal and helpful than people.

3

There was also a higher form of predator stalking the woods a distance away. Maverick could feel the intent to capture, but not for selfish gain. Probably a mother bear, or tama cat, hunting to feed their young.

He settled in to his most familiar cross-legged pose for composing his thoughts, but the predator's thoughts were coming closer, practically deafening among the other desires around him.

He sensed the intent for stealth, capture, and to… use its prey for something of value, but then he felt the distinct desire to learn. Curiosity like this was too complex for a bear or tama cat.

And Maverick flicked his eyes open as he realized he was the prey. The stalker wanted him for information — to learn something from him.

He leapt silently to his feet and whispered, "Stay," to Catch before he pushed past the fur door and emerged into the silent forest. He couldn't hear a single footstep, but the hunter was coming steadily closer, approaching from the top of the cliffs.

What they didn't know, was Maverick could move with equal silence, and he slipped into the trees to circle around behind.

He couldn't imagine why anybody would think to hunt *him* down — Maverick didn't know anything special. Maybe his self-made reputation was making him look more important than he was. He was certainly ready to find out.

He climbed up the side of the rock face without making a noise, and the moment he peeked his head over the crest of the cliffs, the stalker ducked from sight and crawled between the rock crevices to get the drop on him. If not for his power, he'd still have no idea anyone was even here.

Maverick pulled his polished sword from his side and approached cautiously, wishing he had a bow, or at least something sharp and deadly to throw. He should have stolen one of those shanking daggers.

4

He felt the intent to flank him as the thoughts relocated in a flash of movement — the hunter was inhumanly fast.

Fear numbed his veins as he realized it was most likely an Escali — which meant his whole life of dreams and ambitions might just be coming to a close.

The presence darted behind him as Maverick whipped around to see it ten paces away, standing in the open — and he dropped his jaw.

It was an Escali *woman* holding her arms placatingly toward him — a creature that was part terrifying monster, while the other part of her was all stunning woman. Maverick had heard legends of Escalis like this — ones who could woo men to their deaths with just a beckoning of their fingers. He would have been mesmerized by her lithe body and wavy golden hair, but he was more disciplined than that. Maverick kept his sharp eyes on the more monstrous features — the spikes of bone protruding from her elbows, her wickedly sharp teeth, and cloudy, demonic haze to her green eyes.

"It's ok," she said quickly, turning her hands to either side to show herself unarmed. Her words were Escalira, but the intent of them was clear enough they might as well have been spoken in Icilic. "I was told you'd be able to understand me. Can you nod if that's true?"

Maverick nodded slowly as shock and fear coursed through his frozen veins and he clutched his sword for dear life. This would *not* be how he died.

"My name is Glidria," she said slowly, taking a cautious step closer, hands still empty as Maverick readied himself for a cue that she was about to strike. "You are... Mauvrik?"

"Maverick," he corrected softly, watching her closely as he read everything about her. Something was... different.

There was no selfish intent. It didn't make sense. She clearly

5

wanted him, but not for herself.

"Do… you know any Icilic?" he asked, still tensed and waiting. It didn't matter if the intents were selfish or not — she'd come here specifically for him.

"I was warned of this too," she said, "that you would be able to understand me, but I wouldn't be able to understand you. I don't know any of your words."

Maverick couldn't tear his gaze away from her eyes. The green irises were frighteningly cloudy as all the stories had always claimed, but also… *honest.* They portrayed everything she was feeling — her fear, her determination, and her reassurance as she said sincerely, "I'm not here to harm you. I've simply never met a Human. I thought if you could sense my thoughts and know I'm not a threat, perhaps you would be willing to talk to me."

Maverick raised his brows, because that explained the curiosity she felt toward him. He didn't have any special information she needed — she just wanted to know about Humanity.

"I brought you gifts," she said cautiously, reaching very slowly toward her own pockets, so as not to startle him. Maverick could sense she truly wasn't drawing a weapon, and he waited until she held two cloth wrapped items out to him. "They're Escali foods," she said, taking a wary step closer to hand them to him. "Some of our finest."

Every one of his honed senses confirmed that she didn't mean him any harm — he could see it in her stance, hear that nobody was nearby, sense the honesty in her heart, and smell the food she was holding out to him — but sheathing his sword took an act of willful choice. He had to *choose* to trust those senses, more than the fear attempting to panic him.

Maverick sheathed his blade and warily stepped forward to take the items from her hands as she said, "the second is a dagger of our finest craftsmanship. My informants say you keep looking at daggers, but never buy them. I thought perhaps it might be a gift you would appreciate."

Shock may have just permanently widened his eyes as he pulled the cloth off each side to reveal an intricately etched, double-edged blade with a silver hilt. It wasn't the quality of the incredible blade that was making him feel sick — it was that he'd been watched, clearly quite often, and never sensed it.

"I didn't mean to startle you," she said, taking a step back to give him his space again. "I just want to learn from you. Your language. Your customs. Your history. I want to know it all." Maverick wanted to be able to speak, to ask *why*, but she wouldn't understand. "I'll give you time to consider, and then I'll return. In three days," she said, taking another step back. And some strange new feeling in his chest urged him not to let her leave. "If you're not here, then I'll assume you didn't want to meet with me. But..." Her eyes met his, and a nervous jitter flitted through his chest. "I hope you are here. I'd like to know more. I hope to see you."

She retreated further and was almost to the trees when he asked, "Why? Who are you, and what do you want to know?"

She tilted her head like an uncertain animal as her loose, shoulder length hair whipped about in the breeze. And something about the strange movement made him even less eager to see her go. She was full of peculiarities and secrets to unravel. She was exciting and magnetic, with a draw he'd never felt to anyone. Maybe it *was* magic, some sort of seductive enchantment, but that didn't make it any less real.

"Are you asking why? Why your history and customs interest me?" she asked.

Maverick nodded as she pulled her golden locks of hair behind her shoulder to keep them from the tangling gusts of wind. "I come to you because I am Glidria, first sister to our Epic, Prince Avalask, and future queen over all Escali-kind." She broke into a grin at the look of pure shock on his face. "I'll one day be in charge of leading the war against Humanity, and I want to know the minds of those I war against."

Maverick's jaw had fallen entirely open, but the unfamiliar feeling in his chest had taken on a voice of its own and insisted, *don't let her go!*

He wouldn't believe she was real if he couldn't sense her honest intent. Everything about her was sincere, and... selfless. She wanted to be the best ruler she could, for the benefit of the Escalis. He nearly forgot for a moment that he was decidedly *not* Escali, and was actually a member of the species they tended to hunt for fun. The ones she planned to war against.

"I hope to see you in three days," she said, "so I may learn this strange language in which you sing." Glidria vanished into the trees and was gone.

Maverick had never in his life met anyone who scared him so deeply, but he knew without any doubt he'd be back in three days. He was already addicted to the feeling, and a part of him felt like he was in withdrawal. She'd exuded status in every action, and that was something *he* needed to learn from *her*.

He finally turned to climb back down and rejoin Catch in the hideout, and he found himself mulling over how he would even begin to teach the Human language as he scaled the steep rocky cliffs. He pushed the entrance furs aside and found Catch eager to greet him. His companion had sensed trouble and was worried.

Maverick sat and let Catch lean into his side as he grabbed his oldest possession — a worn out grammar and vocabulary book with a tattered cover that had been opened and appreciated thousands of times. It had been his only companion during the years he couldn't bear to be around people. Studying every rule and every pronunciation in the vast lexicon of both Icilic and the regular Human language had kept alive his dreams of someday being somebody worthwhile. A man who spoke well carried a certain air about him that people noticed, whether they consciously realized it or not.

It was one of his deepest held secrets — his love for the rules of grammar and language — and now this Escali had shown up, wishing to learn it from him? Not only an Escali, but one of the legendary women. A member of their royal family. *The future queen.* *What world was he living in?*

He wasn't sure he'd ever believed in fate, but now he couldn't doubt it must be real. How else could the most prestigious Escali in all the world have just come to him, asking to learn about the artform he loved most?

He felt suddenly more alive than ever before in his life, and jittery with nerves. Maybe it was her status that was so exciting, or the fact he would get to revel in the structure of the Human language with a fearfully attractive woman who was eager to learn it. Maybe it was the fact he'd been singled out as someone incredibly special, or maybe it was just *her*. She'd done something to him that had reached the innermost fire of his being, and whatever it was, he couldn't deny he wanted more.

Maybe it was the combination of all of it making him antsy with excitement, but whatever it was, Maverick had never felt such an imperative pressure that he must *not* mess this up.

Fate would never hand him anything nearly as precious as this opportunity again, as long as he lived.

At least, that was what he thought.

9

PART ONE

PART ONE

PRINCE AVALASK

CHAPTER ONE

or all his life, the one thing Prince Avalask had always craved and never experienced was a day off. He was both a prince and an Epic — definitely one of the most powerful young men in the Escali world — and there was simply no respite for the man who could solve any problem.

Well, almost any problem.

He happened to be locked in a deep pit in the ground with one door, no magic, his hands were tied, and he was pretty sure he was about to be executed.

He could barely breathe through his coursing fear, and he paced as far as he could before turning back at the edge of the rocky enclosure to begin his ten-pace journey back to the other wall. Just standing and walking was a strenuous task when there was no magic in the air — he was an Escali, and Escalis couldn't live long at all if they were cut off from magic. It was crippling.

His hands were tied in front of him, so he'd been able tug at the bars across his door until he'd exhausted himself. He'd thrown his shoulder into it until he was too bruised to continue, and even tried to gnaw his teeth into the wood in a vain hope he might be able to make some sort of escape.

He was going to die here.

Epics were primarily combatants. Forget that they wielded every power, and could have easily been builders, and healers, and creators. The Humans and Escalis each got one Epic per generation, and immediately trained them all up into weapons.

Prince Avalask's father, Gramsaf, had spent his entire life battling the Human Epic, Abernathy. Abernathy also had an Epic son named Avery. And while Avery was supposed to be Prince Avalask's lifelong adversary, he actually seemed to think along the same lines Prince Avalask did — that it was an unforgiveable shame they spent their whole lives cancelling each other out in battles, skirmishes, and disputes.

For the first time in history, there was a generation of Epics who stood a chance of possibly getting along, or at least not rendering each other meaningless.

And then Prince Avalask had gone and gotten himself captured.

Prince Avalask usually bit his thumbnails when he was particularly worried, but he'd already chewed them completely away, down to the bleeding nubs.

The Humans weren't going to let him live — not when he could continue to hinder them and eventually have his own Epic son. Killing Prince Avalask meant the end of the Escali's Epic bloodline. It meant Avery would go unopposed. Avery's firstborn son would go unopposed.

The Humans would win the whole shanking war over this misstep.

He heard footsteps and whirled to look at the door, his floor-length black cloak flourishing out behind him with the movement.

It was Avery — the young Human Epic.

Prince Avalask's eyes darted desperately to the closing door, but he knew he couldn't shoulder his way past Avery in this magic-ridden state. He'd be thrown back in and land disgracefully on his rear.

He was going to get *one* chance to talk his way out of this.

Prince Avalask usually had quick wit and a silver tongue, but he found himself short of clever quips now that words meant the difference between life and death.

So Prince Avalask took a long moment to look over his quarry as he gathered what to say. This was just about the first time he'd seen the Human Epic holding still, and Avery watched him closely as well.

Humans were so... *different.*

Their eyes were strangely sharp in color while their teeth were dull and flat. They had no bone-spikes protruding from their elbows. Their childhoods were so slow that even though Prince Avalask was only three years older, Avery looked like a little baby by comparison. Avery was fourteen, with unkempt shoulder length hair the same color as the brown leathers he wore. A fourteen-year-old Escali would usually be fully grown and sometimes married with a kid or two — Avery was just leaving childhood behind.

"Is there someone I can speak to about these accommodations?" Prince Avalask finally asked, gesturing to the bare cave walls around him. He might as well act like himself if these were his final minutes, and he was rather proud he knew the Human word for *accommodations* — the result of studying and learning their language for years now. "You did capture a prince, after all. Is this where princes are usually held?"

Avery glanced about the space and returned an uncomfortable, wry smile. "I'll be sure the next time we catch a prince, he receives the luxury suite."

"I'll be sure to one-up you with something even more grandiose, if you're ever captured," Prince Avalask replied, catching a glimpse of the knife Avery held, the blade nearly half a forearm long. He released an anxious breath and nodded to the weapon. "Is there a

15

chance I could ask you to leave that outside? It *does* rather look like you're here to kill me."

Avery shook his head and said, "We have a few minutes before that happens, and... I've come full of questions."

Prince Avalask took a dreadful step back and warned, "Hey now, there are rules." Really there were only two rules that all Epics observed by tradition. "Epics don't torture each other, or allow it to happen."

He couldn't stop it though. Never in his life had he felt this helpless. Avery could do anything.

"I didn't mean I was here to interrogate you," Avery said, glancing at the knife he held with a hint of disgust. "I just meant... this is the first time we've ever really spoken, and it seems a shame we know so little. I mean..." he glanced around the cave walls in hesitation. "How are you even talking to me right now? There's no magic in this cave at all. You shouldn't be able to comprehend the Human language, use any powers, or barely be able to stand, from how I've heard it."

"Yes, thank you, breathing is difficult too," Prince Avalask added, twisting his numb hands together. "Escalis are knit together with magic, which is why I wanted to speak to your superior about where you're housing me. It's *miserable*."

Avery exhaled with sympathy and said, "I'm sorry." He sounded sincere. "It's the only place that could completely prevent your escape. But... how are you talking to me?"

"Because I learned your language the good old-fashioned way," Prince Avalask replied. "With books, and teachers, and a couple of especially sassy tutors..."

"You mean prisoners," Avery corrected him as he narrowed his eyes. "You mean the people you steal and hold captive for years."

Prince Avalask just flicked his eyes up briefly. "We treat them well, and we let them go after we've learned from them. Whatever

16

cruel fate you think they're suffering, I can assure you it's more trying on those of us attempting to learn from them."

"And why did you never marry?" Avery asked suddenly. "Your childhoods are incredibly short. You should have passed your gifts down to create a new Epic years ago."

"Seven years ago," Prince Avalask agreed begrudgingly, "as my family, and every Escali alive constantly reminds me."

Avery watched him with a puzzled expression, and finally asked, "Why didn't you?"

Prince Avalask exhaled a long, resentful sigh, and said, "I didn't want to keep carrying on the legacy. I thought that…" He hesitated, because it sounded infinitely stupid, given the position he was now in. "I *thought* there was a chance you and I could settle our differences, and either not have kids, or have kids who would never have to fight."

"You didn't want to force this life on a new generation?" Avery clarified. "You were… so certain we could settle our differences, that you held off on adding another combatant to the mix?"

"Don't worry, you're not the only one who thinks it was a stupid decision…" Prince Avalask said bitterly. Nobody had ever been able to understand why he wouldn't want a kid — why he didn't want to put another innocent child through the life he'd been forced to live.

But Avery understood. They'd both seen what the Epic lifestyle did to their fathers — turned them into violent, angry old men. No Epic ever lived into his older years as anything other than bitter.

This could have been different though.

The whole world could have been different.

"Hey… Ten days of vacation will be nice, right?" Prince Avalask asked conversationally. That was the second rule all Epics observed — they gave each other time to grieve, without causing any trouble. Three days if one of them lost a close friend or relative. Ten days if that relative was a sibling, spouse, or parent. It was like a mini cease-fire, giving both sides a sliver of time to recuperate. "You planning to do anything enjoyable with your time off?"

"I hate that we call it that. *The Epics' vacation,*" Avery said in disgust. "As though we've earned a great reward by killing each other's family members. As though I'll be sitting on a beach somewhere while your family takes their ten days to mourn that you're gone."

Avery took a hesitant step closer, and Prince Avalask retreated a step back.

This was really happening. His end was almost here, and it was time to make peace with it.

"Could you... tell them a couple things from me?" Prince Avalask asked, glancing to Avery's tight grip on the knife handle. "Tell my sister it was my *literal dying wish* that she stop doing the very stupid thing she is doing right now." Avery raised his eyebrows as Prince Avalask said, "She'll know what I'm talking about. And tell my father I put up a valiant fight to the very end. Took ten Humans out with me."

Avery let a wry chuckle escape and said, "Our fathers are exactly the same. That would be the final thing I'd ask you to tell Abernathy too."

"And very, very importantly, Avery, tell them that I am absolutely handing the crown to my sister. It does not go back to my father, it does not go to my younger brothers, it's for Glidria."

Avery hesitated, and said, "You have the strangest way of selecting your new leaders." Prince Avalask was pretty sure Avery was stalling for time, not eager to kill him either.

"It's really not that strange," Prince Avalask replied. He wasn't sure why Humans struggled with the concept. "The new Epic always inherits the crown, but passes it on to their sibling so the two can rule together. Then the king and the Epic are always

18

brothers, or a brother and sister in our case. Siblings' thoughts and ideas usually align well, and then the king gets to make the decisions while the Epic carries them out."

Avery nodded and said, "I've seen your sister. She seems competent. Your people adore her, and she speaks like she sees an end to the war."

"Yeah," Prince Avalask agreed as a new wave of anguish doused his already sunken heart. He wouldn't be around to rule beside Glidria, to *end* the Human Escali war and usher in the age of peace they'd been planning since they were old enough to understand they'd rule one day. "She and I were going to do amazing things..."

Avery took another step closer as Prince Avalask backed into the wall, and the Human Epic took a deep breath to steady himself. "Anything else?"

Prince Avalask shrugged and said, "I guess, the standard *tell my family I love them*, and... I don't know... just make it quick. I don't want to suffer."

Avery nodded and just about choked as he said, "I brought the sharpest knife I could find."

"How... thoughtful," Prince Avalask replied, barely able to draw a breath as he pressed his back to the wall and took a few last gasps of air.

He squeezed his eyes shut, and of all the things he could be thinking about — memories he could relive for the last time, family members he wanted to wish well — all he could do was wonder how much dying would hurt. After the initial slice, would it be easy and pain free? Was there anything after this? Would he ever feel again?

"Listen," Avery said, and instead of feeling a sharp piercing pain slicing through his neck, Prince Avalask felt the ties being cut from his hands. "*This* is going to end with you and me."

19

Prince Avalask opened his eyes, but terror had sealed his words right in. "You don't have kids, and I won't either. And maybe, just maybe," Avery said with determination, "you and I can spend our lives doing something meaningful. You and your sister end this war, and perhaps you and I will be the first Epics to make a positive difference."

Prince Avalask couldn't breathe. This was exactly what he'd always been saying — what he always wanted.

"Hurry up," Avery said, pulling the cut ties from his wrists before he looked over his shoulder to the empty doorway. "If we go right now, I think I can get you out of here."

Prince Avalask almost couldn't believe he was looking upon home again as he landed in Dekaron and pressed a hand to his chest in disbelief. He was still standing, still breathing, still alive — and the cedar-and-city breeze of home had never smelled so sweet. An orange sunset glinted off the reflective surface of the Obsidian Tower ahead — one of the greatest Escali masterpieces of all time — and he used a hint of magic to spot his family inside, all huddled around a table as they spoke in quick, low voices.

They were all distraught. Even his Epic father, Gramsaf, who knew almost nothing about love, was frantic with worry. It wasn't only that they were missing a son and brother, it was that Prince Avalask was their defense — their best weapon against magic users. He and Gramsaf, the two Escali Epics, were the only ones who stood a chance against stopping the Human's multitude of magic wielders.

Izfazara, the king, looked over the map and muttered, "They could have stashed him anywhere. We'll have to approach the Human Epics and try to negotiate his safe return."

"Abernathy won't let us buy him back," Gramsaf growled to the map. "He wants nothing but our deaths. We have a limited time to find him before they kill him, if they haven't already."

Prince Avalask could sense the despair from the other members of the family. His mother and the queen both exchanged a look of dread. His younger twin brothers, Savaul and Gataan listened beside Glidria's daughter, Fallistra — the three of them were right on the edge of adolescence and wanted desperately to help, but didn't know how.

Glidria was the one who said, "Abernathy is a monster, but what about Avery? What if we could find a way to approach him on his own, and try to bargain for Avalask's safe return?"

Prince Avalask couldn't help feeling proud that it was his sister who had come up with the best answer.

"We won't play the cowardly fools, approaching them to beg," Gramsaf snarled at his daughter as Prince Avalask pushed open the doors to their living space.

He'd planned to say something funny and disarming, but choked on his easy quip as the whole family turned to see him. His mother beat the others to dart across the room and throw her arms around him, and Prince Avalask took a deep breath as his throat tightened. He suddenly couldn't say anything at all. He just hugged her back and took another deep breath, so glad to be alive he could hardly believe it was real.

"Are you alright?" Glidria exclaimed. "Did they hurt you? How did you get away?"

His father snarled, "It's a shanking miracle you're not dead. What were you thinking, allowing yourself to be captured?"

Prince Avalask let go of his mother in outrage and retorted, "You're the one who let Abernathy grab me! I had Avery taken care of, and you let his father slip away and sneak in behind."

"I taught you to be vigilant and aware of enemies at all angles,"

Gramsaf snapped.

"Gramsaf!" his wife scolded as she stepped back from their embrace. "What are you trying to do? *He's home."*

Izfazara added, "We all know you're happy to see him. Maybe you could find a better way to show it, brother."

Gramsaf hissed a snarl between his sharp teeth and looked to the ceiling as though for patience. "How did you get away?"

"Avery let me go."

The whole family froze at those words.

"Brilliant," Gramsaf growled beneath his breath. "Now we *owe* them. This is a terrible position to be in—"

"Have you lost your Epic senses?" Glidria spoke up. "This is profoundly *good*. Not only is Avalask home, but this may be the first step toward a generation of Epics who don't spend their entire lives warring."

"And this is why you're too incompetent to ever rule," Gramsaf snarled to her in return. "Striking deals with Humans *always* ends in treachery. It's who they are, to take advantage and double cross us. We need a king who leads us to victory, Glidria, not a whiny little queen who leaves us prey to our malicious enemy."

"That's enough," King Izfazara hissed. Gramsaf's wife, Talla, and his brother, the king, were the only two who could reign the older Epic in. "Avalask has already made it clear he intends to give his crown to Glidria. You would do well to learn the arts of support and guidance, Gramsaf, or you'll have no say in her decisions whatsoever."

Gramsaf exhaled a furious sigh and said, "I hope to be long dead by the time she has the chance to ruin all we've built."

Gramsaf disappeared and Glidria fumed angrily, glaring at the space where he'd vanished. This was a conversation they had often. Gramsaf and Glidria disagreed about nearly everything of importance, but she'd be his commander the day King Izfazara

22

passed and Prince Avalask got to choose the next ruler.

"Avalask," Izfazara said, drawing the younger Epic's attention as his heart beat furiously. "Tell me about how Avery came to release you. Did you promise him anything I should know about?"

"He..." Prince Avalask hesitated, but his uncle was the king and needed to know everything that impacted them strategically. "We both said we wouldn't have kids. He doesn't want to pass on this legacy either, of growing into cranky old combatants who hate their own children." Prince Avalask gestured to the place where his destructive father had just stood scolding him for even being alive.

Izfazara exchanged a meaningful glance with his wife, Queen Nori, and Prince Avalask could feel that it was both contemplative and cautionary.

"We may have to talk more about that," Izfazara said, turning his eyes back to his nephew again. "I don't know that *ending our Epic bloodline* is in anybody's best interest."

"And you don't need to worry about being like your father," Nori assured him. "Gramsaf allowed himself to become what he is by giving into his most hateful aspects. We all learn from our parents, but it's up to you whether you learn to be like him, or learn from his shortcomings and become better." She gestured to everyone around them and said, "You'll notice the rest of our family is quite amicable."

Savaul was whispering something to Fallistra beside him, and Glidria snapped her fingers at the three younger kids. "Go wash up. We'll have dinner ready in an hour. Avalask, let's go." She gestured for him to leave with her for the kitchens. "The three of you are welcome to join us," she said to their aunt, uncle, and mother. "Although, Mother, I think we would all prefer if you didn't bring your husband."

Their mother gave an apologetic chuckle and said, "Thank you, but somebody needs to talk a little sense into your father."

23

"We also have a bit to talk about," Queen Nori said, casting a glance at King Izfazara as he nodded his agreement.

"We do," he said, standing to leave with her. "We're glad to have you back though, Avalask. We were all very worried — even your father."

"Yeah," Prince Avalask said with a sharp bark of a laugh, "worried he was going to have to face two Human Epics without me. That was the extent of his concern."

"He was worried," their mother assured him, "he just has an interesting way of showing it."

Glidria rolled her eyes and motioned for Prince Avalask to join her as she finally left.

Cooking was something he and Glidria did together often — whenever he wasn't out fighting Humans, or healing the sick, or protecting Escalis from natural disasters, or assisting the lost, or meeting with Escali leadership, or taking his translation classes... It was true he would never get a day off as long as he lived, but he always tried to make time to cook with Glidria and sit down to eat with Savaul, Gataan, and Fallistra. Since they'd rule one day as the queen and the Epic, and it was important that they stayed caught up and on the same page with events happening around them.

He took a deep breath of the delicious kitchen air, trying to feel normal again when anger and relief to be alive still had his hands shaking. "So, what are we making?" he asked, wanting to rid himself of the feelings altogether. There was nothing but the kitchen to worry about — just the combining of ingredients and the enticing smells that would waft from the ovens. It was a safe, calming place.

"Mother's vegetable-roast and venison rolls," Glidria replied. Prince Avalask reached to grab the nearest chopping knife, but something about it froze his reach before he could wrap his fingers around the handle. It looked too similar to the knife Avery had

24

held.

Glidria noticed his hesitation and grabbed the knife without feeling the need to comment, or ask what was wrong with him.

"Arrange and season the vegetables, will you?" She began chopping orange gella roots and passed the thin pile of rounds to him. "And tell me everything," she added as Prince Avalask lined the bottom of the nearest pan with the spicy, sliced roots and she moved on to chop zucchini.

He took another deep breath and said, "I was so afraid, Glidria. Avery was going to kill me, and would have gone through with it if I hadn't been able to communicate with him. I can't tell you how glad I am that I joined the translation program three years ago. It just saved my life."

"I know where you're going with this," she said, shooting him a sideways squint as she passed over the sliced zucchini and started on the onions. She lowered her voice to emulate Gramsaf's and rasped, *"No women in the translation program. It's improper."*

Prince Avalask exhaled a laugh and said, "You know Izfazara would stand up for you. He's the one with the authority, and I'm sure he'd see the value of you learning all you can about Humanity." Glidria shrugged with disinterest, and Prince Avalask added, "I've made some of my best friends in that program. And it will give you the chance to learn from real Humans—"

"I appreciate all it's done for you," she said, passing the onions as she moved onto slicing the venison into thin strips, "but my own translation program has been working out rather well for me, I'll have you know."

Prince Avalask sighed to the counter, because he knew exactly what she was talking about. "Glidria... That Human you keep spending your time with will be rich beyond his wildest dreams when he decides to turn you in. I *hate* that you keep seeing him."

Glidria gave an easy laugh in response and said, "Believe me,

Avalask, he is *not* hurting for money. Turning me in for a bounty is the last thing I would need to worry about."

Prince Avalask gave a disgusted scoff and said, "He's rich because he hunts people for a living."

"*Bad* people," Glidria clarified, "but in the four years I've known him, he's never been a threat to me, Avalask. And he really *could* have used the money before he joined the Zhauri two years ago. He's worked incredibly hard to get where he is." Glidria was clearly thinking fondly back on the past four years before she suddenly looked up from her slicing, tilted her head in thought, and said, "I want you to meet him."

"*No*," Prince Avalask retorted immediately. "Because then you're going to think I approve of the situation. *And I do not approve*," he hissed.

"Oh, come on, I value your opinion." She returned to her slicing.

"You already have it. I don't like him."

"You haven't met him," Glidria insisted as she passed him the strips of venison to season. "And light the cook stove, would you? Unless we're planning to eat everything raw tonight."

Prince Avalask reached a hand behind himself to summon a blaze of flames into the stove.

"I'm to meet him at the full moon, which is tonight," Glidria said. "I want you to come. I'm serious."

Prince Avalask groaned and worked the seasoning into the meat before him with much more force than necessary. There was already a chance it was too late for her to break off her ties to this Human, so… maybe Prince Avalask should make an appearance, and give the man a reminder of who he was messing with. If anything happened to Glidria, the entirety of Escali kind would join together to retaliate. She was as widely adored as her Epic brother.

They were going to make an amazing team when she took the crown. Between the two of them, he *knew* they could end the

26

Human-Escali war. Then he would finally get to take a day off like he'd always dreamed. Come to think of it, when they ended the thousand-year war, he was going to go wild and take a whole week!

And as much as he hated to admit it... the Human she was so fond of might actually be in a good position to help them.

"I will come meet him," he finally conceded. "But I'm not going to like it."

"I think he'll be able to charm even you," Glidria said through a grin.

"Well aren't I in for a treat?" he grumbled.

Prince Avalask

Chapter Two

Glidria usually snuck out of Tethi Rakna to meet Maverick. She knew how to easily navigate the underground labyrinth and slink, unnoticed, into the rocky northern mountains to see him.

But since she'd come to Dekaron with the rest of the family in their concern for Prince Avalask, it was up to him now to jump them up to the northern hills where Maverick awaited.

He and Glidria landed gracefully in a dark outcropping of jagged stones, all frosted over in ice, in a location near her Human. The freezing northern winds were mercifully still, and the two moons overhead were bright enough to cast shadows off the scrubby trees growing from between the rocks. Prince Avalask found himself suddenly grateful for the warmth of his black fur cloak and pulled it around himself as he took a deep breath of the freezing air and let it escape between his teeth.

"Let me talk to him first," Glidria said, "and wipe that scowl off your face. If you're not going to give him a chance, then go home."

Prince Avalask flashed her a sarcastic, sharp-toothed smile and Glidria gave him an amused sneer in return before she turned to approach the friend she'd been meeting with for years now. Prince Avalask used magic to watch her climb over boulders and maneuver between them before she finally reached a small valley carved into the stone hills, where Maverick sat waiting by a crackling orange fire.

His entire face lit with an elated grin as she approached.

"Welcome back," he greeted her, and Prince Avalask could sense him holding back a giddy laugh, he was so happy to see her. He held up a thick, leather-bound book, and said, "I think you'll be proud of me. There'll be no more telling me I write like a fish after you see this, Ria."

Prince Avalask wanted to throw up in his mouth. She let him call her *Ria?*

Glidria raised her eyebrows with challenge and said, "I will be very surprised if that is the case. But before we get into your terrible penmanship, I do have a slight confession to make..."

He gave her an unconcerned smile and said, "I already know. You brought your brother."

She gave him a guilty grin in return and asked, "Is that alright?"

Maverick just shrugged, looking too happy to be terribly worried. "I guess it depends on whether Avalask decides to rip me apart or leave me intact."

"That's *Prince Avalask*," he corrected the Human, appearing beside his sister. He expected Maverick to shy away, or at least look somewhat frightened, but the Zhauri had no fear in him. He looked Prince Avalask up and down, searching for his intentions as Prince Avalask did the same.

"It's good to finally make your acquaintance," Maverick said with a disarming smile. He stepped forward with a hand extended. "I'm Maverick, of the Zhauri Brotherhood."

"I know who you are," Prince Avalask retorted. "I'm the one who has to deal with your scent all over my sister —"

Glidria punched him hard in the side, and he rolled his eyes. "You promised," she hissed beneath her breath.

"I don't like you," Prince Avalask said in a much more cordial tone. He reached to politely shake the man's hand as Maverick still showed no signs of fear. "But, I acknowledge that you're probably not going away any time soon. So… here we are."

Maverick seemed to find him funny and exchanged a smile with Glidria before saying, "I like your sister very much, Prince Avalask."

"Yes, go speak your suave words at somebody else—"

"Enough to tell her that her older brother is hiding something."

"What?" Prince Avalask let go of Maverick's hand and narrowed his eyes. Could he have truly sensed it?

No. It wasn't possible…

"What are you hiding?" Maverick asked, as though a matter of mere curiosity. But his steely eyes seemed bore right through him — regardless of the fact he was the Epic.

"What *are* you?" Prince Avalask asked, throwing a mental barrier around his mind that his father wouldn't be able to shatter. But something about Maverick's gaze was unnerving. He truly had sensed Prince Avalask's deception.

"Every Zhauri brother has powers stronger than an average mage," Maverick explained. "Roughly five times stronger. And my power is to sense intentions."

"I know that's your power, but… I wasn't even thinking anything deceptive."

"You feel latent guilt, for hiding something of importance from someone you care about."

Prince Avalask's jaw just about came unhinged with surprise as Glidria tilted her head in confusion.

"What would you possibly have to hide from me?" she asked incredulously as she slipped to Maverick's side to take his hand. "I mean… I'm the one introducing you to the Human I've spent my last four winters with. You have something more secretive than that?"

30

Prince Avalask didn't know what to say. This was neither the place, nor the company with whom he wanted to share what he knew.

He *was* going to, just… *not now.*

Glidria frowned at her brother and said, "You and I have never kept secrets from each other. What do you have to tell me?"

"It's not something I can talk about here," he replied as he looked the Human mage over with disdain.

Glidria turned uncertainly to Maverick and asked, "Can you tell what it is?"

Maverick shook his head and replied, "Only that it's important."

"Listen," Prince Avalask said in a low, dark growl. "I have nothing to say to you, Human, except that you had better be *exceptionally* careful. If I ever find out you've crossed my sister—"

"I'm not the one harboring secrets here," Maverick replied in a cool voice, not revealing one bit of fear or anger. "Every thought and intention I have is entirely honest, as you can very well tell. You're the one I would advise her to look out for."

Prince Avalask scowled in return, lacking a suitable comeback that wouldn't sound like a child stomping their foot and shouting, *no, you're the shady one!*

"I need to leave," he said, maintaining his calm. "Glidria, call for me if you need me. I'll talk to you when you get home."

"Good meeting you," Maverick said politely as Glidria glared and Prince Avalask leapt away.

PRINCE AVALASK

CHAPTER THREE

lidria usually stayed with Maverick for a couple days when she went to visit him, which left Prince Avalask to his own chores and duties as he waited for her to return home.

He had a few skirmishes to attend to — one near Dekaron and the other near Treldinsae — where he quickly appeared to help the Escalis tear into the opponents attacking them.

These were the times he didn't question whether or not his enemies needed to die — if they were attacking Escalis, the decision was made.

Gramsaf quickly joined him in each location and the two of them fought side by side to tear out the throats of their attackers — it was the honorable way to kill, even though killing with magic was much faster and cleaner.

Avery and his father Abernathy showed up to oppose them at each location, and the four Epics broke into the type of battles Escalis liked to tell their children about at night. Avery and Prince Avalask locked themselves into combat as though their encounter had never happened, but Prince Avalask knew he had an ally in Avery. It certainly didn't look like any conventional alliance as they vanished and reappeared, took their battles into the sky, threw and blocked lightning, and completely cancelled each other out of the battle below — but Prince Avalask could feel it was there.

Gramsaf and Abernathy fought with greater frenzy, each nearly driven mad with the want to kill the other, even though neither of them ever came away with a scratch.

Prince Avalask always stayed after events like this to heal whoever needed it, and Gramsaf left him to it. They didn't have much to talk about anyway, and his father didn't have the patience or the disposition to enjoy healing in the slightest. Prince Avalask appreciated being able to actually help people, as opposed to only being able to negate the Human Epics, and he also enjoyed being left to do it alone.

He was exhausted by the time he dragged himself to his translation class, where the head of the program, Onnik, said nothing about his tardiness or his absences. Onnik was extremely organized — really, to the point of obsession — and he had a tidy stack of papers to hand to Prince Avalask upon his arrival.

"Everything you've missed," he said curtly, and Prince Avalask nodded back as he flicked through the papers in his hand. Prince Avalask understood that every language *had* to have grammar rules, but Humanity had taken theirs to the heights of insanity, making sure only the most masochistic Escalis would ever want to learn the Human language.

It was all *subjects*, and *objects*, and *tenses*, and every rule had a hundred exceptions. Every vowel could be pronounced ten different ways. The whole language was a mess.

"You missed the difference between conjugating past tense verbs and past participles," Rallek said as he slid past Prince Avalask to hand a book to Onnik.

"I'm sure Rallek can fill you in," Onnik said as he handed Rallek a new book to read. "I'll be assessing your comprehension at the end of the week, both of you. Prince Avalask, you just come when you can."

"Thank you," Prince Avalask said with a brief bow before he and

Rallek proceeded toward their own classes.

"You just tell me when you have a free moment, and I'll catch you up," Rallek assured him, exhaling a chuckle at the exasperation that crossed Prince Avalask's face.

"I don't know the meaning of *a free moment*," Prince Avalask replied. "If I ever come to see you, it means I'm prioritizing it over literally every other event on this continent that could use my help."

"Oh believe me. I'll be sufficiently honored by your presence," Rallek replied in a tone of unimpressed sarcasm. Prince Avalask loved that he had friends here who weren't afraid to be sarcastic. Rallek was one of his favorites.

"You know, I stepped into your class a few days ago, since they hadn't seen you in a while."

Prince Avalask exhaled in amusement and said, "I hope my unruly bunch gave you a warm welcome."

Rallek broke into a grin and said, "I almost died laughing. Your Humans are *funny*, and I'm going to steal them if you don't start showing up more often."

"I will fight you for them," Prince Avalask replied with a smirk as he stopped at the door to his class.

"It's not fair," Rallek protested as he reached his own door. "My tutors just sulk and cower when I try to talk to them."

"You've told them they'll be released right? And that they're not in any danger?"

"Of course I have. I just got defective ones."

"Maybe it's their translator who's defective," Prince Avalask suggested as Rallek made an ugly face at him and pushed his door open. Prince Avalask entered his own small *classroom*, which was connected to a sleeping room in the back, and he was immediately greeted by his three favorite Humans.

"Prince Avalask, where have you been?" Flora exclaimed as he closed the door behind himself. "We were starting to worry you'd never be back."

"We're. So. *Bored!*" Sass exclaimed as she flopped dramatically into her chair. Their simple learning room only had a table with three chairs behind it and one for him on the other side. He'd never been into the back room where they lived and slept.

Flora was a heavyset young lady, with a kind face, wavy dark hair, and a worrying heart. Sass was just about as opposite as a woman could be — with short cropped silver hair, dramatic flair in every action, and a gaze that could pierce metal when she got fired up.

"Are you telling me Rallek didn't keep the three of you entertained?" he replied in mock outrage. "It's the *only* job I left to him."

"Rallek sucks," Sass replied with a great eye roll. "He wanted to talk about things like *the weather.*" She gestured to the three of them with an exaggerated huff. "Do the three of us *look* like we've seen the weather lately?"

"Or like we'll ever get to experience it again?" Darin added in a low brooding voice. Darin was Prince Avalask's one killjoy in the group, a young man with sparse hair and just about no chin, but Prince Avalask still liked the guy. He felt especially accomplished whenever he could get a laugh out of him.

"Well, there's no need to miss out," Prince Avalask said with an easy grin. "Darin, you just tell me what weather you want to experience, and I'll bring it right here to you."

Darin glowered in return as Sass exclaimed, "Don't give him that power! He'll order up a bunch of gloomy rainclouds to make us all miserable with him."

"Why don't you tell us what's been going on with you?" Flora suggested kindly. "We didn't mind Rallek, but he didn't tell us anything that was real, or that even slightly mattered."

35

"Whereas you give us all the good details," Sass said, rubbing her hands together in anticipation. "So *spill*. Why haven't you been coming to visit?"

"Because *I* have had a terrible week," Prince Avalask replied as he broke into a deep sigh and told them about a few of the skirmishes he'd attended and people he'd helped.

The three of them were definitely his prisoners, like every other Human who was taken for the translation program, but they also doubled as friends and therapists. He'd learned much more than the Human language from his three tutors in the year they'd had *class* together. The three of them would be released in less than a year, after he'd completed the program, and he expected he'd miss their time.

He told them of everything going on, except of course, Glidria's affair with Maverick. Nobody could know about that. And he finally got to the point in the story where he admitted, "*Then* I went and got myself caught."

Flora gasped, and said, "You didn't."

"How unfortunate for you," Sass drawled. "Wish we knew what that felt like."

Flora nudged Sass with her elbow and said, "That must have been very frightening."

"It was," he agreed, "but the fact I could speak Human saved me. I'd be dead now, if not for all the help the three of you have given me."

"Oh wonderful," Darin muttered. "I get to die knowing I helped save the Escali Epic."

"Hopefully of old age, and knowing that I am very grateful," Prince Avalask replied easily.

"And... you're alright?" Flora asked hesitantly. "They didn't hurt you, did they?"

"No, I'm fine. Epics have a strict code to treat each other decently

36

whenever we're captured."

"You make that sound like it happens often," Sass said.

He shook his head. "This was my first. Gramsaf and Abernathy have both been caught multiple times though. And then my father had the nerve to yell at me for being careless…"

Sass leaned in, and used her most gossipy tone to whisper, *"He didn't."*

Darin groaned and looked up to the ceiling. "They're never going to let us go with how much he tells us."

"Shh! It's Prince Avalask — he'll just wipe all the juicy parts from our minds before we go. Now give us the details," Sass said. "Spare nothing. We're dying."

They knew exactly what Prince Avalask thought of each of his family members, which made the surprise all the more shocking as the door behind him flew open unexpectedly.

Prince Avalask leapt to his feet as Gramsaf stood in the doorway with a distinct expression of disgust on his face. "We need to leave," he told Prince Avalask. "An opportunity has arisen."

Sass raised her eyebrows as she looked him over. "This must be Gramsaf?"

Prince Avalask cursed Sass's fearlessness as Gramsaf turned his cold gaze to her and hissed, "Why do your Humans know my name?"

Sass seemed to take his unfriendly demeanor as a challenge and quipped, "Oh, he *is* irritable."

Gramsaf's hand shot out, and his magic forced all three of them out of their chairs and into an abrupt kneel. Their sharp gasps of pain as their knees crashed onto the stone floor prompted Prince Avalask to action as he counteracted the magic holding them roughly down.

"Leave them alone, and tell me where we're going. I'm ready," he said.

Gramsaf looked over the three kneeling prisoners and said, "Just so the three of you know, I was adamantly opposed to the change in rules that allowed our translation subjects to be released alive. And rules can always be overturned." He turned dangerous eyes back to Prince Avalask and said, "We go, now."

Gramsaf grabbed his son by the shoulder and leapt them to an empty trail near the Human city of Kellington.

"What did you find?" Prince Avalask asked, looking warily around them. A small cabin sat nestled into the trees ahead, nearly impossible to see in the dim light. The whole thing was covered in vines, camouflaging it from anybody who happened by.

"Stay out here, and stop anybody from interfering. There isn't time to explain."

Gramsaf turned invisible as Prince Avalask did the same, and he took up a post where he could see the cabin's front door.

His father was brutal and unlikeable, but Gramsaf *did* care about protecting the Escalis and had wisdom regarding the Humans that Prince Avalask couldn't deny. When his father told him to come, to fight, or to stand guard, he did so without asking questions.

Prince Avalask heard the door to the cabin creak slowly open, and then heard a female scream from inside. And in a matter of seconds, Avery and Abernathy appeared outside the house and bolted inside.

Prince Avalask darted after them as a guttural cry of outrage erupted from the house, and he knew something was terribly wrong. He got through the door just in time to see Gramsaf and Abernathy collide in an explosive detonation of powers. But Avery wasn't helping his father, he was knelt over a dead Human woman on the floor, and was trying desperately to heal her.

"Ma! Ma, wake up!" he was saying over and over, and Prince Avalask's heart turned black and sank as the magic in his hands faded.

38

They'd killed Avery's mother.

Abernathy's wife.

Any chance of the Epics being more than enemies had just died with her.

"Nooo," Avery whispered as Abernathy and Gramsaf exploded the back wall of the house and took their deafening, snarling showdown outside. Prince Avalask darted forward to see if he could help, but she was beyond healing. Avery looked up in utter disbelief and breathed, "You killed her."

"Avery, I didn't know—"

"I *just* let you live," Avery breathed as he turned horrified eyes back to the woman on the ground. "I should have known... I should have just *listened.*" Avery cursed himself softly and set a hand over his mouth in horror as Prince Avalask stood and took a step back.

"I'm *sorry.* I didn't know. I just came along, and I..."

He didn't know what to say. He hadn't even *asked* who they were coming to kill. It would have changed everything if he'd just asked.

He heard more shouting outside, and then a blinding flash of light exploded and shook everything in the house as he turned and threw an arm up to shield his eyes.

The bright explosion blew past, and Prince Avalask looked out to see his father convulsing on his back, lying on the ground as he writhed in silent agony. And Abernathy was gone.

Prince Avalask darted to Gramsaf's side and reached to see what was wrong, but he couldn't figure out where to even begin helping. He couldn't tell where the pain was starting, or what was causing it. Avery stumbled out of the destroyed cabin to see that his own father was nowhere to be found.

"Abernathy?" his son called out in shock.

Avery looked around in bafflement then moved to pick

39

something up from the grass, and Prince Avalask's heart leapt into his throat at the sight of it.

It was a small glass orb, filled with swirling and snapping black shadows and lit by tiny, purple strikes of lightning.

It was a curse. It meant that Abernathy was dead and had left behind a terrible shadow of himself to seek his revenge. He could not believe all of this was happening right before his eyes.

"Avery," Prince Avalask said slowly. Avery held the glowing black curse up to look at it. "You have to destroy that, right now. That's your father's soul trapped in there."

Avery gave him a long, hollow look before he turned his eyes back to the flickering darkness contained within his palm. Both his parents were dead. That seemed to be all he could comprehend.

"This... is twenty days," Avery whispered. "I want ten for each."

"Avery," Prince Avalask replied in despair, "you can have all the time you —"

The Human Epic vanished and Prince Avalask gaped after him. He looked down to Gramsaf in disgust, then picked him up and jumped him back to Dekaron. He landed in his parent's room and dropped Gramsaf roughly onto the large bed along the wall.

Something was terribly wrong with his father, but he couldn't find the energy to care. He wanted desperately to find Avery and tell him how truly sorry he was, but Avery had taken great care to conceal himself, and Prince Avalask couldn't locate him.

Prince Avalask

Chapter Four

Glidria finally returned home several days later. Prince Avalask was already in the kitchen, starting on their dinner when his sister entered with folded arms and raised eyebrows. She had no idea how wrong a time this was to be trying to pick a fight.

"I'm ready for that secret now," she hissed through bared teeth.

"And I am not in the mood for your attitude right now," he snapped back. He was still fuming with rage at all that had just been ruined.

Glidria broke into a scowl, but the retort was uncharacteristic enough that she knew something was wrong. "What's the matter with you?" she demanded.

Prince Avalask slammed the clay bowl full of berries onto the counter and accidentally shattered it. He gritted his teeth as concern finally came to Glidria's face.

"I thought Avery and I were going to be different," he growled to the remains of the bowl beneath his fingers. "I thought we'd be able to settle our issues and end the Epic feud, and I just helped kill his mother *and* father."

Shock finally filled his sister's face. "Why would you—"

"Gramsaf didn't tell me who we were killing," Prince Avalask snarled. "He just said to watch his back, and I did. Now Epics will continue to war and feud for the rest of time."

Glidria took a long moment to let that sink in before she moved over to grab a rag and brush the shattered clay remnants off the counter.

"Avalask..." She shook the shards into the rubbish box at their feet, and looked back up with reassurance. "I know this isn't what you wanted, but if Abernathy's gone, that means you and Gramsaf will finally be able to catch Avery. We'll have a two against one advantage, and he'll *finally* be subdued."

"Abernathy left a curse behind," Prince Avalask said suddenly.

"A curse?" Glidria repeated in surprise. "A real, *actual* curse?"

"I saw it. The thing looked exactly like the books described, and I know Abernathy was angry enough to leave his soul behind to haunt us. He'd just watched his wife die. That thing was real."

Glidria frowned and twisted the rag in her hands. "What do you think it will do?" she asked, her voice softened with worry.

"I think it's doing something to our dear old father already. He's lying in bed, delirious. I've never seen anything like it before."

Glidria's frown darkened. "You didn't want to stay and look after him?"

"Not particularly."

"Is he going to be alright?"

"Will either of us mourn if he isn't?" Prince Avalask spat back.

Glidria looked thoughtful, and moved to start layering their baking pan with the berries he hadn't managed to smash.

"I'm sorry. That things between you and Avery have crumbled," she finally said. "A lot of good could have come if you didn't live up to the expectations to be sworn enemies."

Prince Avalask nodded his furious agreement, and then left her to the cobbler as he grabbed the chopping knife without flinching this time and angrily began chopping onions for their stew. Every chop bore the brunt of his frustration as the knife dug further and further into the chopping counter beneath.

42

"I'm still curious to know what you thought of Maverick," Glidria said, in a blatant attempt to change the subject.

"I don't like him," Prince Avalask declared, "and there *are* Humans I like, Glidria," he added quickly, cutting off her protest. "Lots of them. Just not him. He reeks of schemes and manipulation."

"You just hate that he's kissing your sister—"

"I *wish* you'd stopped at kissing him," Prince Avalask groaned, lowering his forehead into his palms in disgust.

"*Avalask*," she scolded.

"Don't *Avalask* me! You're pregnant. That's what I needed to talk to you about."

"What?" Glidria's eyebrows shot into her hair. "I can't be pregnant."

"Well, you are," he said, throwing a hand up. "I didn't want to say anything, because there was still a chance it wouldn't take. But… it's there, and it's growing. Congratulations," he added dryly. "I can't wait to break the news to our father."

Her jaw fell open. "You wouldn't," she whispered in horror. "He'll kill me."

"I'm not about to run and tell him, but…he's going to notice at some point," he said, gesturing to her still-flat stomach. "You could always get rid of it. I'd help you—"

"No." She set a hand protectively over where the beginnings of a baby lay. "I need to talk to Maverick."

She turned to leave, but he reached for her arm and said, "Wait."

She whirled on him with the same scowl and demanded, "*Why?*"

"You can't leave the house right now. Avery's going to be looking for revenge against our family—"

"I don't care if Avery's set the path to Maverick on fire. I need to talk to him—"

"Listen, I will help you hide this," he said, almost not believing the words were coming out of his mouth. "I can get you through this whole pregnancy undiscovered if you promise not to tell Maverick you're having his baby."

She spat back, "You are out of your mind—"

"Glidria, there is something terrible about him. I can't tell you what it is, but I can *feel* it. You have to stop seeing him." She glared as he said, "I would never ask something so difficult of you if I wasn't truly worried."

Prince Avalask felt something like screaming at the edge of his mind, and tore himself away from the current conversation to look out over the continent and see who needed his help. It wasn't a stranger — it was Savaul, struggling in the hands of a Human as two others stood over the body of their own mother, Talla, on the ground.

"There's been an attack," Prince Avalask said, and without any hesitation or explanation, he leapt across the continent to Dekaron to save his brother from the Humans about to kill him too.

Prince Avalask

Chapter Five

Prince Avalask killed the three attackers the moment he landed, and he pried Savaul out of the grasp of the third before the Human's body hit the ground. Savaul was hyperventilating as Prince Avalask set him quickly on his feet and dashed past him to their mother on the floor. They'd snapped her neck — completely severed the connection from her mind to the rest of her body.

There was no healing something like this. She was gone as quickly as Avery's mother had passed.

"You can fix it," Savaul said with a face full of hope as he grabbed Prince Avalask's shoulder and squeezed as tight as he could. "I know you can. I've seen you do more incredible things."

Prince Avalask just shook his head and reached to pull Savaul into a tight hug. "It can't be fixed, Savaul. Don't look any longer. This isn't how you want to remember her."

Savaul dissolved into sobs against him and tried to choke out that it was his fault, but couldn't get the words out through his anguish.

It's not your fault, Prince Avalask spoke into his mind as he hugged him tighter.

She hid me, and I watched it happen, Savaul cried back in thought as his shaking finally began to calm. He was settling into *norithe* — the sleep of the mourning. Prince Avalask could feel it happening

45

as the despair began to shut him down.

This was something all Escalis did when emotions became too overwhelming — their higher thoughts and functions turned off, and they'd fall into a sleep that allowed them to process the pain. They called it *norithe*.

I was too afraid to help her, Savaul said in his thoughts. *I didn't defend her. I stayed hidden until it was too late. It's my fault...*

All Prince Avalask could do was hold him and share thoughts of support and love as Savaul's mind finally shut down completely in grief.

Prince Avalask looked back down to their mother in disbelief. Was this fate trying to play a cruel trick on him, to kill his own mother days after he'd had a hand in killing Avery's? Was there any chance this was truly just a coincidence, or was it a consequence of the curse he'd just seen?

The reality hadn't seemed to hit him yet. She was dead, but he didn't believe it.

Nobody would have blamed him if he'd collapsed into *norithe* as well, but he didn't have time to stew in his grief. He was the older brother — he had things to do. He had to take care of the rest of the family in the wake of despair that was sure to follow.

Prince Avalask picked up Savaul and located Gataan out in the courtyard. Prince Avalask leapt out to Gataan and gave his younger brother quite the scare as he spotted his twin in Prince Avalask's arms.

Gataan rarely had anything to say — he usually let Savaul do the talking and happily sank his teeth into anyone who offended his brother — but he bared his teeth and demanded, "Who did this to him?"

"Come with me," Prince Avalask said, holding a hand out to take Gataan with him. He couldn't leave anybody behind.

Gataan was a violent, destructive force to be reckoned with, but

46

he did follow his family's instructions when they were given. He reached a hand to grasp Prince Avalask's, and the Epic leapt them up to the obscure back crevices that led to Tethi Rakna.

"What's happening," Gataan asked, his teeth still bared as though they might be attacked at any moment.

"I'll explain when we get to Glidria and Fallistra," Prince Avalask replied as he trotted toward the city and Gataan kept up with him.

He made sure to hold Savaul securely, to keep his head from rolling as they proceeded through the city's back gates, into the mountain fortress, and all the way to where Glidria was braiding her daughter's hair into a war updo, as though they were about to go into battle together. They were chatting pleasantly until Prince Avalask entered the room and Fallistra bolted out of her chair.

"What's happened?" she demanded, approaching to see Savaul unconscious as Prince Avalask lowered him onto Fallistra's bed. Fallistra and Savaul had always been close — always discussing and scheming new ways to get information out of the older members of the royal family.

Prince Avalask looked up to Glidria and said, "He'll be alright, but Mother's dead. He watched it happen — thinks it's his fault for not defending her."

Everybody in the room froze in a stupor as those words sank in. Mother was dead.

Glidria set a hand over her open mouth as Gataan narrowed his eyes in fury.

"She was killed by Humans?" he spat in disgust.

Prince Avalask nodded as Glidria looked to him with suspicion.

Just after Avery's mother was killed? she thought to him. *This is supposed to be some sort of coincidence, that our own mother dies right after?*

I know, it's too close to be coincidence, he agreed. *But Avery wasn't there. He's using his grace days to mourn his own parents. I don't sense his presence or his scent anywhere related to the scene.*

"Does Gramsaf know?" she asked. "Or Izfazara and Nori?"

Prince Avalask shook his head and said, "I grabbed our brothers and came straight here."

Glidria pulled up a chair to sit beside the smallest of them. "Oh, Savaul," she said, brushing his black hair back from his face.

"He should be able to hear you," Prince Avalask said softly.

"We know," Fallistra told her uncle, folding her arms over her stomach as she watched Savaul's silent sleep. "Mother and I both mourned in *norithe* after my father died. It's a state of pure feeling, but you can tell when others are nearby, and the general feel of what they're saying."

Prince Avalask nodded and said, "I need to tell Izfazara, Nori, and Gramsaf. Can you take care of him?"

"Of course, go," Glidria said. "And Avalask," she said before he turned to leap away, "It's not your fault either. Don't you dare let yourself think so."

He gave her a wry smile in return, then leapt away.

Panic and alarm spread across the whole continent as Escalis learned the Epic's wife had been killed. Gramsaf had just been starting to recover from his strange incapacitation, but he curled in on himself as the grief put him into a coma, and Prince Avalask finally came to terms with the fact she was really gone. Savaul slept for several days while Glidria and Fallistra took turns watching over him. Gataan never left his brother's side, and seemed to want their attackers to come back from the dead so he could tear them apart in retaliation.

Gramsaf finally awoke after a week of recovery to find he couldn't use his powers. He suddenly couldn't light a candle, hear

48

a thought, or lengthen his own shadow. Every shred of Epic magic was gone, and the Escalis fell into despair as they found out they were down to only Prince Avalask for their defense against Human magic.

The whole continent was still in a state of mourning when two weeks later, in a completely unexpected lash of fate, Queen Nori dropped dead from an extremely rare form of heart failure.

The news struck the royal family first and hardest. Prince Avalask and Glidria found themselves cooking dinner for the family that night in a dull stupor, not knowing what to say to each other. Savaul was just finally beginning to eat and take up his normal daily lessons again after the death of their mother. He retreated back into silence as they learned of the queen's passing, and Gataan and Fallistra stayed with him in their own shock.

"Is anyone looking after Izfazara?" Glidria asked as she slowly pulled the feathers off the chicken they were about to roast. Their poor uncle had loved Queen Nori with every bit of his heart.

"Gramsaf and Aunt Ildra are there," Prince Avalask replied, thinking over the set of three siblings who had almost nothing in common. Izfazara always ruled with kindness and wisdom, Gramsaf was the angry and bitter Epic, and Aunt Ildra had always been a bit on the loud and eccentric side. But they came together in solidarity when it mattered. Prince Avalask was glad they were both there to help his uncle through the grief.

Except three days later, Ildra was leaving Tethi Rakna when a freak landslide cut through the mountain passes and buried her. The entire party traveling with her was killed.

"Avalask, what is happening?" Glidria asked in a whisper as they arrived in the kitchen together, too distraught to cook anything.

"It has to be that curse Abernathy left behind," Prince Avalask replied numbly. "He'd just lost his wife. Gramsaf and Izfazara lost

49

their wives almost immediately after."

"What about Aunt Ildra? She never married. She wasn't anybody's wife."

Prince Avalask gave a brief half-shrug, at a loss for an explanation that made sense.

"You have to find Avery and get him to break that curse," Glidria said hoarsely. "Who knows who it might target next."

"I've already been looking for him — I can't find him," Prince Avalask replied. Avery hadn't surfaced once since losing his parents.

Glidria met his eyes and said, "Maverick could find him—"

"Glidria, we don't need Maverick's help."

"This is what he and the Zhauri *do*. They can find anyone," she insisted.

He scoffed in return and said, "I will find Avery without the help of the Zhauri, and I'll figure out how to end this."

Prince Avalask searched the continent, looking for a hint of the Epic's scent, or a Human stupid enough to talk about harboring him. He looked in the most desperate corners of Humanity to see if Avery would show up to help any of the people he was supposed to watch over, and all he ended up accomplishing was saving a couple Humans who needed the help of an Epic to survive. He didn't usually save Human lives, but he wasn't opposed to it if they seemed like innocents.

He couldn't believe that he and Avery were the only two left, now that Gramsaf's powers were gone and Abernathy was dead — only existing in the form of his remaining curse. Their Epic grandfathers and great grandfathers had all killed each other, each of them ending up more bitter than the last. Prince Avalask could see exactly how and why the bitterness happened, and he could

50

already see it happening to him and Avery.

After a few days of searching for the Human Epic, Gramsaf came to him with a lost look on his face. "Avalask," he said, his voice scratchy while dark circles had formed beneath his eyes. His words had no fire or venom at all as he said, "I need you to help me locate your grandmother. Nobody can find her."

Prince Avalask's blood just about froze as he reached out to find Grandmother Silna, the one who'd married Gramsaf's Epic father, Ravnak. She'd given birth to Gramsaf the Epic, Izfazara the king, and Ildra their slightly odd sister, before she lost her husband to the age-old Epic feud.

Prince Avalask searched every corner of the continent as Gramsaf said, "she was last seen in Troskora, leaving to travel up to Drukmir. She has to be around there somewhere. Her sister was with her too."

Prince Avalask searched the entire area, looking for her friendly spirit and the sparky attitude she'd retained well into her older years. "I can't find either of them," Prince Avalask whispered.

Gramsaf just shook his head in despair and said, "It's got to be that curse Abernathy left behind. What else could be doing this?" Prince Avalask nodded numbly as his father said, "It's only after the women, Prince Avalask, and if your grandmother and her sister are truly dead, that means there are only two females left in the family that curse could possibly target."

Prince Avalask nodded again in shock, but then something finally went right.

He sensed Avery out attacking a group of Escali travelers.

"I have to go," he said, suddenly vanishing to reappear beside Avery. Prince Avalask shielded the Escalis and went after Avery as the Human Epic vanished and reappeared on a cliff, overlooking the caravan he'd just harassed.

"Avery," he said cautiously.

"How nice to see you again, Prince Avalask. It's been too long," Avery replied. He looked exhausted and broken.

"I've been looking for you."

"All to say you're sorry, no doubt."

"I *am* sorry," Prince Avalask insisted. "I didn't know it was your mother in that cabin, or I never would have let Gramsaf anywhere near her. I didn't want you and I to live the rest of our lives as enemies. Neither of us wanted that."

Avery stared long and hard at him before he said, "It's a real shame, what's been happening to your family lately."

Prince Avalask stiffened for a moment before he finally said, "What did your father curse us with? Every man in our family loses his wife?"

"You're close," Avery replied. "They'll lose every woman they love. Sibling love counts just as much. How is your sister, by the way?"

Prince Avalask gaped in shock. This wasn't Avery, to taunt him with the looming death of someone he cared about. This was the first time the Human Epic had ever been so cruel.

"Avery, you have to break it. I'm sorry for what happened. Haven't you taken enough in return?"

"That curse was my father's will," Avery replied casually. "I feel no desire to nullify his final wishes."

"There has to be something I can do. Something I can give you," Prince Avalask said, feeling desperate. He couldn't let Glidria die next. "What do you want?"

"To see that curse play out," Avery replied with a look of disgust. There it was. The Epic bitterness. "It was created so your entire family would have to feel the pain you caused mine. I'm not breaking it."

"Avery—"

"Enjoy your last days with your sister."

Avery turned and vanished, and Prince Avalask took a deep breath. That curse was *not* going to kill Glidria or Fallistra. He knew what he had to do. He released his deepest breath and then located the last man he wanted to approach, but the only one who could help him. And then he leapt and reappeared in the northern forests.

Prince Avalask approached the camp of the Zhauri Brotherhood where firelight flickered in the dark and glittered off the snow dusting each cedar bough.

The mercenaries had a Human man tied to a tree right beside them, just far enough from the fire that it's warmth couldn't reach him. Prince Avalask could feel his terror, could feel him freezing, and hurting, and the Zhauri Brotherhood sat around the fire without any concern, talking and laughing among themselves as they left him to stew in his fear.

Everything about them was terrible.

Maverick, I need to speak with you, Prince Avalask thought to him.

Maverick heard the Epic's voice clearly in his mind and knew immediately who he was.

"We have a visitor," he told the other Zhauri, and they all fell quiet to look in the direction Maverick's eyes had turned.

Prince Avalask took a deep breath and strode toward the group as though he harbored no fear at all — even though these were a few of the people in the world who *did* put real unease in his gut.

"Now this is a surprise," their leader, Navvad, said with raised brows. Prince Avalask was probably one of the only people in the world able to set this group of hunters on edge as well. "What brings the great Prince Avalask to our fire?"

"I need to speak with Maverick," he said. "In private."

Maverick glanced to Navvad, and said, "Anything you say, I'll repeat back to my brothers. If you need something, they'll be part

53

of the decision making. You might as well speak here."

The man tied to the tree struggled and moaned in pain, and the Zhauri had no empathy whatsoever. He was too far beneath them to be considered a person, and his cries of agony invoked no feeling in them.

"What did this poor man do?" Prince Avalask asked, gesturing toward their victim.

"Nothing in particular," Navvad replied, glancing back as though noticing their guest for the first time in a while. "He knows a few things we need to know. We'll likely release him after we're done here, if he's cooperative enough."

"You're telling me he hasn't even done anything wrong?" Prince Avalask replied in disgust.

"We also said we'd likely let him walk away," Maverick added with a frown. "Which is more than kind on our part. He's a nobody, Avalask. No one would miss him."

And those were the words that made him rethink this entirely.

Those were the words that completely summed up why Maverick made him feel so uncomfortable. Even other Humans weren't people to this man. Everyone beneath him was just a tool to be used and discarded, and Maverick considered this world beneath him.

He does love your sister, a small voice in his head reminded him. *It doesn't matter who he is, you need his help.*

"How much do they know?" Prince Avalask asked, nodding to the other Zhauri around the fire.

"About Glidria?" Maverick clarified. "Everything. I've kept no secrets."

"Then I'll tell you all. Abernathy used his death to cast a curse on our family, and I need your help to break it."

This seemed to surprise all of them, and Navvad broke into an easy chuckle. "That must be some curse for you to come to *us* for

54

help." He grinned casually and added, "You have come to the right people, but it will be very costly."

"I can afford any price you ask," Prince Avalask replied, "but I need that curse found and broken quickly. It's killing all the women in the royal family, and there are only a few left."

"*It's what?*" Maverick repeated, rising to his feet as fear flooded into the man's veins. At least he had some sort of feeling to his name.

"Glidria and Fallistra are the only two left," Prince Avalask said, "but I don't know how much longer that will be the case. I wouldn't have come here if the situation weren't desperate."

"Tell us everything," Maverick demanded. "We'll destroy it for you."

"Maverick," Navvad warned in a low voice. "We'll need to discuss—"

"There's no time," Maverick replied as an unforeseen panic widened his eyes. "I'm calling in my *Ilthit Nocknul*. We'll do it for free." Navvad shook his head with reluctant acceptance. Whatever an *Ilthit Nocknul* was, Prince Avalask was glad they seemed to take it seriously. "I need you to tell me everything you know," Maverick added quickly. "Who cast it, where at, and who was the last person you know to have seen it?"

"I can tell you exactly who has it," Prince Avalask replied. "You have to track down Avery, the Epic."

Navvad turned a darker look to Maverick as he said, "Avery is not a man I particularly wish to cross."

"And Glidria will be the queen of the Escalis," Maverick retorted. "Having the Escali queen owe us a favor is a spectacular position to be in." Navvad still looked hesitant, but Maverick turned back to Prince Avalask and asked, "Where is Avery now?"

"I have no idea. I can't find him," Prince Avalask replied, glad to see Navvad looking to Maverick as though he already had a few ideas brewing.

"We'll find him for you," Navvad said, looking back to Prince Avalask again. "And we'll destroy that curse as well."

"You just keep Ria safe in the meantime," Maverick told him. "We may need time for a task of this magnitude."

"I will," Prince Avalask replied, "I'll keep looking too and let you know if I find anything. I doubt you've ever hunted for an Epic before."

"We haven't," Maverick replied, "but we're the Zhauri Brotherhood. We can catch anyone."

Prince Avalask

Chapter Six

It was three months later that Prince Avalask landed in the mountain cliffs and sprinted toward Tethi Rakna as his black cloak billowed behind him. The Escali guards along the cliffs could tell it was him, but the fact he was sprinting put a panic into all of them as they tried to see what was after him.

It's nothing to worry about, he projected the thought to every guard he startled, and even to one guard who'd fallen asleep near the city gates. He would have stopped to reprimand the woman if he'd had any more time, but he didn't.

He bolted through the courtyard, then into the mountain fortress, and he reached Glidria, Izfazara, and Gramsaf in time to see his father smash a glass onto the ground in rage. "You were never gone long enough for bonding," Gramsaf snarled. "This *can't* be happening."

Izfazara just had a hand over his mouth in disbelief as Gramsaf turned furious eyes up to Prince Avalask. "You had a hand in this," he growled beneath his breath. "How did she do it? And who is the shanking father?" Gramsaf's eyes darkened as he turned back to Glidria to tell her, "You are an insult to your mother's memory, tarnishing her name in promiscuity and loose virtues—"

"You're pathetic," Glidria hissed in return.

"And you are banished from this family," Gramsaf snarled.

57

"You could not have possibly been a greater disappointment, Glidria. Leave this city and never approach us again."

"I. Will. *Not*," Glidria retorted, her face red with rage. "Tethi Rakna is the safest place for Fallistra and I to survive this curse. I will stay here until the day this baby is born, and for as long as I want after!"

"And who do you think you are to give that order?" Prince Avalask added furiously. "You're not the king, the future king, or even the king's Epic anymore. *Everybody* in this room outranks you."

"Izfazara has let the two of you get away with far too much, but this is where he'll draw the line," Gramsaf said with confidence. "You've broken the most sacred of Escali laws, Glidria. There's no coming back from that."

Glidria turned to Izfazara, who was usually so calm and understanding, but he still appeared broken from the passing of Queen Nori. He looked devastated now as he shook his head to Glidria and whispered, "This will ruin you."

Glidria's shoulders finally slouched as the king said, "This will be the scandal of the decade, Glidria, that the future queen is pregnant and not married. I just... how could you have been so careless? It would have been fine for you to marry again after Lonnir died. You could have bonded and had more kids, you just had to marry the man."

"I would have if I could," Glidria insisted as a hint of despair cinched her brows. "He would have been thrilled, but it wasn't an option. And... I never meant for this to happen," she said with a glance down at her growing belly.

Prince Avalask heard his uncle's thoughts whirring and knew the king was going to figure it out any second. Because babies couldn't happen without intimacy, and intimacy between Escalis couldn't happen without triggering bonding, and bonding took anywhere from eight to fourteen days. It was the physical, chemical process that tied Escali mates together forever, and it couldn't be skipped.

But Glidria had never been absent from their family meetings for nearly long enough to have bonded with an Escali. Izfazara was right at the edge of the answer, but he couldn't quite grasp it.

"It's some commoner, isn't it?" Gramsaf demanded. "You knew we wouldn't approve of a marriage, so you went and got yourself pregnant behind the back of every law."

"No," Izfazara said as disbelief widened his eyes. "Glidria…. tell me it wasn't a Human."

Glidria finally shrank back a step as Gramsaf let a bark of a laugh escape and said, "That's not possible."

"He wouldn't have had the corresponding pheromones to keep bonding going, so it would have been short," Izfazara breathed. "And that's why you couldn't marry him, or tell anyone. You wouldn't have cared if it was a commoner. It had to be *much* worse for you to cover it up, *you* who fears almost nothing."

A blank look crossed Gramsaf's face, as though his daughter had just died in front of him. Prince Avalask was certain their father would have handled her sudden death much better.

"It's not possible," Gramsaf repeated, turning his eyes to Glidria in some sort of stupor. "You've never met a Human."

"One might assume, since I was never allowed to join the translation program," she agreed through a sneer. "I went out and found my own Human instead. He taught me their language, and taught me all about how they think and act. He taught me their customs and their ways, but he was also a friend to me after Lonnir died. And as the years passed, that friendship grew more affectionate. I never meant for it to happen, and if I could have married him, I would have."

Gramsaf and Izfazara had both fallen silent in bewilderment

59

now, but Prince Avalask could feel the violence brewing in his father. This was not going to end well.

"I know this baby is an inconvenience," Glidria said, "but it could also be an incredible asset to us. We can raise it here, and then the father can take it to the Humans to learn too. By the time it grows up, we might have someone who can help bring the Human-Escali war to an end."

"Who is the father, Glidria?" Gramsaf asked in a low whisper.

Glidria sneered and said, "He's powerful — too powerful for you to kill. He'll be able to make our child into somebody with the Humans."

"You would be very surprised who I can and cannot kill," Gramsaf said dangerously.

Glidria released a sharp laugh and said, "His name is Maverick, and he's a member of the Zhauri Brotherhood. You'll never touch him."

Prince Avalask cursed silently that she had to be so brazen about that part.

"Glidria," Izfazara whispered in horror, "you could not have possibly picked a more dangerous Human."

A part of Prince Avalask wanted to chime in and agree with that sentiment, but it made no difference now. "There is one other benefit to consider," he contributed instead, stepping up to stand beside his sister. "This will finally give us another magic wielder to help defend against the Humans. And if the father is any indication, he or she will be incredibly powerful."

Izfazara was in utter shock, and said, "It'll have Escali blood and the powers of a Zhauri."

"That baby will bring about our ends," Gramsaf hissed. "You gave it a blood tie to the entire royal family. If the Zhauri get their hands on it, they'll use it to destroy us."

Glidria laughed again and said, "Maverick doesn't want to

60

destroy—"

Gramsaf ran at her with every intent of killing the baby she carried, and her too, if he could manage it. Prince Avalask had a shield around his sister before Gramsaf got anywhere close, but his goal was clear to everyone in the room.

"You're wrong, and I'll prove it to you," Glidria snarled as she sank into a defensive stance, preparing to fight him. Prince Avalask used his second hand to magically hold her back from charging forward.

Prince Avalask heard the tiniest creak from the door and turned to see Glidria's golden-haired daughter listening in from outside. He made sure Fallistra saw his gaze and knew he'd spotted her, but he didn't rat her out to anyone else. She backed slowly away from the door.

"This baby will grow into whatever we raise it to be, and yes, it *will* be a threat to you, Gramsaf," she spat. "Because you never want to see this war end, and I am going to be the one who ends it, with Maverick's help. And I'll have no place for people like you in the world I'm building, so know that the moment you come near me or this baby, I'll kill you. This is your only warning."

Izfazara seemed to be paralyzed with disbelief as Gramsaf hissed back, "It's you or me then, daughter. Because I won't let you destroy everything your ancestors toiled to provide. This is your warning as well. Rid yourself of that baby, or I'll kill you both."

"I tire of this," she announced. "Avalask, let us be off."

She turned and strode from the room, and Prince Avalask was not about to let her leave by herself. He shot a look of warning back to Izfazara before he followed Glidria out and quickly caught up to walk beside her.

He could feel that her heart was racing as quickly as his own.

"That went about as well as expected," she said as he nodded numbly.

61

"We should leave the city," he replied. "I'll take you somewhere our father can't find you."

"No, this is still the safest place to escape the curse," she replied. "And I am truly more than ready to kill Gramsaf if he comes near me. This is where I want to remain."

Prince Avalask didn't think Tethi Rakna was any safer than any other city, with their raging father contained within the walls, but she knew the risk. It was up to her.

"Avalask." He turned to meet her determined eyes, and she asked, "Do you believe me when I say I can turn this baby, and this whole situation into a good thing?"

He bit hesitantly at his thumb nail, and they covered half the hall before he finally replied, "I believe in you. It's Maverick I don't trust. If you can cut him out of the plans, then I think this baby could change everything."

"You don't have to trust Maverick," she said with reassurance. "Just trust me when I tell you I know what I'm doing."

He let a long sigh escape, because he did trust her. She was more than competent.

"Glidria... do you still think you can be queen after all this settles?"

She looked right back at him and said, "Avalask, this baby changes nothing in my plans. It simply gives me a new advantage. The Escalis can have their meltdown over the scandal of it all, but we'll persevere. Between you, me, and Maverick, we'll create a world where Humans and Escalis cease their warring, and we could not have a better omen than the coming of this baby. Whoever he or she is, they'll help us in a way nobody else has ever been able to."

Fallistra

Chapter Seven

allistra moved silently through the frozen northern tundra and approached a moonlit tendril of campfire smoke as terror raced in her veins. A duskflyer's melancholy song echoed around the rocky terrain as ice crickets chirped happily from the shrubs and sparse evergreens. She moved with graceful stealth, and tried to plan how to announce herself to the group of killers.

Zhauri. The word felt strange, but she felt her best course of action would be to walk into the camp, and confidently call them by their name. *Zhauri. I am Fallistra. I've come to ask your assistance.*

"Are you Fallistra?"

Fallistra shrieked in surprise, silencing the crickets as she whirled around to see a man in intricate grey clothes and a white fur cloak. Fallistra leapt up from her stealthy crouch and darted back from him.

"Yes," she said, skittishly looking all around the trees for more of them. She couldn't *believe* he'd snuck up behind her. "You... Did you just read my mind?"

He returned a disarming smile and said, "No. You just look incredibly like your mother."

This had to be Maverick. The young man had a thick build, flat white teeth, and the strange sharpness of Human eyes in a steely blue.

63

"What are you doing out here? Alone?" he asked with a strange calm that put her on edge. He knew she was by herself. What else did he know?

"I came to ask for your help," she said, her nerves almost too overpowering to talk.

"Where is your mother?" Fallistra watched as his face sank into an unreadable calm, and she realized he must already know something was wrong. He was worried.

"She's in Tethi Rakna. She thinks it's the safest place for us to escape Abernathy's curse, but..."

"It *is* the safest place, until we're able to break it," Maverick agreed. "We're getting closer, but what else is wrong?"

Fallistra nodded, and was pretty sure he didn't know about the baby yet. She wasn't quite sure how to break such news.

"Tethi Rakna's not safe anymore. Gramsaf found out she's pregnant, and he's going to try to kill her to keep the baby from being born."

Maverick froze for a long moment, and his voice cracked as he repeated, "Pregnant?"

Fallistra nodded, and twisted her hands together as she muttered, "It's... yours."

Maverick's jaw fell open. He finally broke into a breathless chuckle of bewilderment before he set a hand over his mouth and whispered, *"Oh no. This is bad."*

"I really think the safest place for her now... is with you," she said softly. "Even the Escalis know how powerful the Zhauri Brotherhood is. I was hoping you might protect her."

Maverick's face remained emotionless for a long moment. "You must be cold out here," he finally said, breaking into a pleasant smile that startled her. "Why don't you come join us at our fire? You can tell the story to the rest of the Zhauri as well."

Fallistra froze, her mind whirring through the options. She was

64

safer out here — able to bolt away if Maverick tried to grab her. But if she really wanted their help, she *would* have to ask all of them to assist her. That had been her plan all along, to approach their camp. It would be easier for Maverick to introduce her, than for her to introduce herself.

"Alright," she agreed, her voice trembling as he courteously gestured for her to walk beside him.

She wasn't sure she'd ever been so afraid.

"Just so you're aware, Zhauri don't attack their guests," Maverick said conversationally, his mastery of Escalira impressive. "If a Zhauri brother invites you to join them by the fire, that means it's safe."

"Thank you," she said beneath her breath as the flicker of the warm flames began to dance through gaps in the dense foliage ahead.

Maverick led the way, and Fallistra just tried to keep breathing as they stepped into the tiny clearing where the rest of the team had set up camp. The other four men stood as they stepped out of the trees, and Maverick immediately began to speak to them.

Fallistra was dreadfully disappointed to realize his words were all Icilic, the less used, northern language of the Humans. She didn't understand a single word as the other four listened. Her guts tightened even further as she began to dread what he might be telling them.

The Zhauri spoke to each other in low voices, and her skin prickled in warning as each looked her over. She was on the verge of bolting away and calling the entire endeavor a mistake when Maverick set a hand on her shoulder. "Come and sit."

The Zhauri began settling back into their chairs, but one remained standing and gestured courteously for her to take the stump he'd been sitting on when she first arrived.

"*Zhif dan irzn Avalask norna?*" The man at the fore of the fire asked, studious eyes still fixed on Fallistra.

Maverick took his hand off Fallistra's shoulder and moved to join his brothers at the fire. "You'd best come sit and explain yourself," he told her casually. "I can translate anything you say."

"Do they speak regular Human?" Fallistra asked, still standing rigidly.

"Yes," Maverick said, breaking into a mild frown. "I didn't realize you could."

"Not perfectly, but Mother has taught me quite a bit. I'll do my best."

Fallistra gathered her courage and finally seated herself in the circle, sitting up straight and proper. Her mother could look regal in any circumstance, and Fallistra tried to channel that confidence as she met their eyes and said in Human, "Thank you for listening." She actually thought she was quite good with their language, but her voice still felt small. "My mother is..." she didn't know the word for pregnant, and improvised, "she holds Maverick's child. Her father is... angry, and wishes to kill her for it. If she stays in Tethi Rakna, I fear he will kill her. If she leaves Tethi Rakna, Abernathy's..."

"Curse," Maverick said for her.

"Abernathy's *curse* may kill her. It is a... danger to me too, but I took the... risk to come ask if you can help. She could be safe with you. Safer than she is in Tethi Rakna with Gramsaf. Safer than anywhere else where the curse can target her. We don't have any magic users except Avalask who can protect her."

The man who she sensed was the leader leaned in to say, "You want us to break into Tethi Rakna and *steal* her?"

That wasn't exactly how Fallistra had been imagining it, but... it would do.

"Imagine what that would do for our reputation, Navvad," Maverick said with a cunning grin. "If people know we're able to capture the Escalis' next queen at our leisure, who won't hear of our prowess?"

The leader, Navvad, replied, "We can't protect her and hunt down this curse you're after. You'll have to pick one or the other, Maverick."

"We can," Maverick insisted. "We'd just have to split up. We'll leave the strong ones behind to guard her and send the smart ones out to get the curse."

"Heeeyyyyy," another of the Zhauri warned in a low tone, the one with the low ponytail of black hair.

"You know exactly which one you are, Hakkrui," Maverick retorted, seeming mildly amused by his protest.

"The Zhauri's strength is in our unity," Navvad warned him. "Split us up, and we just become your average group of mercenaries."

"Our strength is in our wit and discipline," Maverick disagreed. "We will still have those when we're split. And pulling off this feat will give us an unforgettable place in history. That's a better payout than any job we've ever done for coin."

Navvad watched him for a long moment, then switched back to Icilic to speak much more quickly.

Maverick listened intently, then replied in rapid Icilic as well. Fallistra could recognize a name here and there when he used them, but the rest was a jumble of meaningless words — pretty and melodic, almost with a hint of song to the language, but meaningless.

The Zhauri spoke among each other. Maverick was clearly trying to convince the other four to take this on as he spoke the most, and their leader, Navvad, finally switched back to the more common Human language to ask, "If we decide to come steal her out of Tethi Rakna, do you have a way of getting us into the city?"

"You already know of the labyrinth, don't you?" Fallistra

67

replied.

"Yes," Maverick said. "That's how your mother gets out to meet with me. Would you guide us through it so we can take her away?"

Fallistra took a deep breath — this was *why* she'd come.

"Can you promise me she'll be safe if I take you to her?"

"Both of you will be," Maverick told her as he looked to Navvad and got a nod of approval. "You can come too. We'll keep you and your mother safe and secure while Navvad and I go out to break the curse."

"Then yes," Fallistra replied with a nod. "I'll take you through it."

Prince Avalask

Chapter Eight

Sleep was always difficult for Prince Avalask when the world constantly clamored for him, needing help, and healing, and protection, and aid in their battles, and information, and of course there was still the curse he had to find and destroy. He'd slept for a few restless hours and woke in the morning in a sweaty tangle of blankets. He reached to make sure Gramsaf was safely away from Glidria, and then reached to see Glidria was...

Gone.

He bolted out of bed and searched the whole city for her. If something had gone wrong, she should have called for him. Where could she possibly be?

Prince Avalask jumped into her room and took one whiff of the air before he knew exactly what had happened.

Maverick.

He'd been here with several other Human men — obviously the other Zhauri — and she'd left with them. Of course she would — she trusted Maverick without reservation.

Prince Avalask was furious for only a moment before he had to admit to himself this was exactly what he needed. Now he could focus his greater effort on breaking the curse while Maverick kept her safe. He didn't like the Zhauri, but he did trust them to protect Glidria well.

He tried to track them down, but couldn't locate them, or his sister. Again, he didn't like it, but it was probably for the better. Maybe the curse couldn't find her this way either...

Prince Avalask couldn't track them with magic, but the Zhauri had a scent strong enough that he could follow them just about anywhere. He followed the smell of the Humans through the corridors of Tethi Rakna until he came to the secret trapdoor that led into the labyrinth below the city.

And that's when it donned on him.

Fallistra.

She'd been listening outside the door. She'd heard everything, taken matters into her own hands, and led the Zhauri into Tethi Rakna to help protect her mother.

She certainly was Glidria's daughter.

Prince Avalask was about to set out on his quest to keep looking for Avery, but flicked his attention down to check on his brothers first. And he found Gramsaf sitting with Savaul and Gataan, speaking as they both listened eagerly.

Prince Avalask vanished and reappeared in their doorway as Savaul asked, "Why does Izfazara allow the Humans to keep existing? Every Escali should leave their home and march against them. We're stronger, but we keep letting them destroy everything we love."

"That's what Humans do," Gramsaf told him as Gataan watched through narrowed eyes. "They pillage and steal, they rampage through our lands killing anyone they come across, and it's essential that we have a king someday who doesn't show them endless mercy." Gramsaf looked up and met Prince Avalask's eyes as he said, "There are those who believe we should seek peace, but they're fools and cowards, Savaul. If we don't crush Humanity, they'll destroy us."

Prince Avalask folded his arms and said nothing in return. Not every Human was inherently evil, but with all the loss his family was facing, it sure was hard to stand up for them.

"When you're king, it'll be up to you to remember what they are," Gramsaf said.

"Glidria is going to be the queen," Savaul said. "And she thinks peace with Humanity would be better."

"She won't be the queen if this curse gets her," Gramsaf told him, and Savaul's face paled at those words.

"Knock it off," Prince Avalask growled. "Nothing is happening to our sister, Savaul. That curse will be broken before it ever finds her."

"But if it does destroy her, and you do become our future king," Gramsaf said, "don't ever forget who killed her. Our whole race deserves revenge. We deserve a king who sees that, and will act on it."

"We couldn't forget who did this," Gataan said, giving Savaul a dark, brooding glare. Savaul returned the look with a determined frown of his own. If he ever became king, Humanity was going to pay for all they'd done, and more.

Prince Avalask went after Avery whenever he could find him, but his tactic changed. There was nothing in the world he could say to get that curse back from the Human Epic, but if he could capture him, he was certain he could coerce the location of the curse out of him. These were the exact circumstances that might drive him to break the Epic's tradition of decent treatment. He might have to.

He'd never actually tortured anyone before, and wasn't sure he could even bring himself to do it, despite Glidria's life being on the line. He would probably be better off calling in the Zhauri who were masters of the art, but Prince Avalask didn't have to make a decision until he'd actually caught the Epic. It was possible Avery could be reasoned with, without stooping to such lows.

Avery figured out his intention quickly, and became suddenly more elusive — incredibly difficult to find, and willing to flee rather than stand and fight. Prince Avalask absolutely couldn't pin him down.

Prince Avalask was staking out the Dragona, the Human's school for training magic users, and also a great source of controversy among Escalis everywhere. There were those who wanted to attack, since it was the training grounds for Humanity's most dangerous killers, but at the same time... it was a *school*, full of children. Izfazara stood strongly in the camp of belief that attacking things like schools and hospitals was wrong, no matter who was in them.

But it didn't stop Prince Avalask from moving invisibly through the Dragonan caves, looking for thoughts related to Avery or the curse. There were plenty of adult mages here who were clued into Humanity's strategic knowledge, but none of them were thinking about anything helpful.

Prince Avalask ran across one girl in her mid-teens who looked perfectly content sitting alone in a corner as she sketched a quill mindlessly across a sheet of parchment. Her name was Anna, and he'd seen her before — she was hard to miss with thick curls of fiery red hair resting on her shoulders. Nobody had ever seen anything like it, hair that was naturally orange, and nobody had been surprised to find she wielded fire in a capacity nobody had ever seen before.

Her strength rivaled the Zhauri's.

She was thinking about Avery, but in an unexpected way — pondering over what the next Epic would be able to do if he had Avery's powers and her strength in wielding them.

She'd spent quite a long time to write out a list of powers in elegant calligraphy, each gift surrounded by intricate details that represented them. The word *FIRE* had been illustrated spitting sparks, and with flames licking up the sides of the word. Beside it she'd written, *Burn entire cities to the ground.*

The word *ICE* was frosted over and placed among snowflakes with icicles dripping off each letter. And beside it she'd written *Freeze the Breathing Sea.* Beside the word *SHIELDS*, drawn within a protective, shimmering barrier, she'd written *Unbreakable. Unstoppable.*

The thought crossed Prince Avalask's mind that maybe Avery wouldn't stick to his word anymore — maybe he *would* have a kid and disregard the promise they'd made to one another. And if he did it with this powerful witch of a girl, Prince Avalask could only guess what sort of destruction the world would suffer. An Epic who could burn cities down with a snap, freeze the Breathing Sea, influence the minds of thousands of people at a time... He shuddered to think of the day they may have to combat such a threat.

He reached to subtly influence Anna's thoughts to the last time she'd seen Avery, and the answer was yesterday. He'd come to visit her. The two of them were friends, but she didn't know where he'd disappeared to.

"You must be Anna."

Prince Avalask startled at the sudden, unexpected appearance of Maverick and three of the other Zhauri, and Anna calmly stood and picked up her parchment to wave it in the air long enough to dry.

"And you must be here with purpose, to have sought me out this way," she replied as she rolled the parchment back into a scroll.

"Yes," Maverick told her with a pleasant smile, "but there's actually somebody else in this room I need to speak with first."

Prince Avalask's face would have darkened into a scowl if he weren't invisible.

What do you want? And why are there four of you here? Prince Avalask demanded as Maverick looked straight to where he stood. If there were four Zhauri here, it meant only one guarded Glidria and Fallistra.

Your sister has grown terribly sick, Maverick replied as Prince Avalask snarled in outrage. The sound startled Anna as she took a step back in uncertainty and brought a flame to her hands. *I thought our mages would be able to heal her,* Maverick went on quickly. *I took her to some of the best, and had very convincing conversations with each of them, but they can't figure out how to help her.*

So you thought you'd set off to find the curse, and only leave one person behind to guard her?

We left Hakkrui, who is more than capable of holding an army back. Fallistra's not a bad defender either.

Prince Avalask lanced into Navvad's undefended mind and immediately found where Glidria and Fallistra were holed up with Hakkrui.

Steal her back if you think you can help her, Maverick said as soon as he sensed Prince Avalask's intention to vanish and grab her. *You don't have to attack. Hakkrui will let you have her.*

How kind of him, Prince Avalask thought back before he leapt and reappeared in an obscure area of the northern forests. A cozy shelter had been built into one of the mountain caves, and Hakkrui was inside with Fallistra and Glidria. Prince Avalask pushed the furs in the entryway aside and stepped in to see the three of them gathered around an uprighted stump serving as a tiny table between them.

Glidria was lying out on a cot, watching as Fallistra and Hakkrui each held a set of cards in their hands. Fallistra laid a card between them.

"Are the three of you enjoying yourselves out here?" Prince Avalask asked, drawing their attention. Nobody seemed worried, or the least bit guilty that they'd run off and left him without any hint of where they'd gone.

"Immensely," Fallistra said, staring hard at Hakkrui as he flashed a confident smirk in return. "I'm about to win for the first time since coming here."

"That's a lot of confidence for someone with only a few low pairs left," Hakkrui replied, laying a card between them as he grinned. Prince Avalask had no idea how the rules worked, but Hakkrui's thoughts said he knew Fallistra was going to win, but he could still beat her if he could convince her to surrender her hand. Leave it to the Humans to invent a game where the best liars won.

Fallistra was staring hard at the cards she held, second guessing if she really could beat him.

"Are you alright?" he asked Glidria, feeling a terrible pain emanating from her. Her entire body was chilled and aching as spasms of pain shot from her spine.

"I'm fine," Glidria replied, propping herself strenuously onto an elbow to sit up just a fraction. "I'm actually enjoying these card games quite a bit. Maverick taught me to play a long time ago, but there was never any point playing with him — the mind reading sort of ruined the fun."

I can feel your pain from here, Prince Avalask thought to her.

Believe me, I can feel it from where I am too, she shot back. *But Fallistra's beside herself with worry. Don't give her any more concern to bear.*

Prince Avalask moved to grab one of the makeshift log-chairs and sat beside Glidria to take some of her pain without Fallistra noticing. It was one thing to numb pain, to make it bearable, but to take and bear somebody's pain was a much more loving gesture. It gave the person under his hands the ability to feel *alright* again, instead of feeling nothing. It didn't seem like much, but people could feel what he was doing for them, that he was giving his own

75

comfort in exchange for their suffering, and nobody ever went ungrateful for such an act.

Fallistra was losing confidence in the cards in her hand as Hakkrui taunted, "Lay them all. You *know* you have the winning combination. Put them all down."

What's wrong with you? Prince Avalask asked solemnly as Glidria took a deep breath and relished feeling pain-free.

As if I know. I just know everything hurts. I can't even get up without this agony in my back knocking me back down.

Maverick said the Human mages couldn't even figure out how to fix you.

They also don't have a lot experience examining Escalis, she thought back.

You know I'll do everything I can to fix it, but… I have to know what's wrong, Prince Avalask told her. *If our healers can figure out the problem, I'll be able to help.* He looked at her and asked aloud, "Are you ready to go home."

"Yes, home sounds nice," she agreed.

Hakkrui looked up from their cards and warned, "It may not be safe to move her."

"Thank you for your concern," Prince Avalask snarled in return.

Hakkrui shrugged in indifference and turned to stare Fallistra down again. "You going to risk it all or not?"

She finally condensed her fanned out cards into one pile and pulled them back from the table. "I'm out. Pile's yours," she gave in.

"Good move," he told her through a smirk, even though he'd just manipulated her right out of her own victory.

"We'll have a rematch someday," she told him as she stood to grab her things.

Hakkrui gave her a taunting salute and said, "I'll look forward to it."

Prince Avalask couldn't take the girls to Tethi Rakna — there was no way he was about to carry Glidria through the mountain crevices to get her into the city. They needed to come up with a way for him to jump in and out of Tethi Rakna one of these days, because the front gates took *forever* to open, and having to walk through the back gates every time was becoming a great pain.

He took her to Treldinsae instead. It was the closest city, but also one of the most dangerous, as Treldinsae and Dekaron were right in the midst of Human territory. Nobody would expect him to have brought her to Treldinsae.

Fallistra stayed with her mother as Prince Avalask went back out to summon the best healers he knew. They argued and discussed and worked with him to try to figure out what was wrong, but at the end of the day, all they could diagnose her with was an overdose of Abernathy's curse.

Prince Avalask didn't leave her side for weeks, not for a single emergency across the whole continent, but she went into an early labor anyway, and their entire team of healers, midwives, and the Escali Epic together couldn't figure out why it was going so wrong.

Fallistra stayed in the room and had taken on a permanent shade of pale as she watched her mother's condition go from bad to worse. The curse was doing something to destroy her, and nobody could figure out how to stop it.

Prince Avalask couldn't leave, but projected the thought out to Maverick, *You're almost out of time. You need to break that curse right now.*

And Maverick had thought quickly back, *We're almost there. I'll have it destroyed by tonight.*

Prince Avalask could sense he was busy, and didn't have much time to devote to eavesdropping on the Zhauri to see how they were doing it. All he had to do was keep Glidria alive until tonight.

But everybody in the room could see that wasn't going to be an easy task. She kept fading in and out of consciousness and in a moment of clarity, she grabbed her brother's shoulder and rasped, "Bring Savaul and Gataan."

Prince Avalask was back with them within minutes, but landed outside the door of her room. He grabbed them both to quickly explain, "She's having a baby, and… she's very sick. She wants to see you two."

"She can't be having a baby," Savaul replied, just as a statement of fact. "She's not married."

The innocence of that reminded Prince Avalask of just how young they both were, but a look of shock spread suddenly across Savaul's face as a possibility occurred.

"Did the Humans do this to her while they had her?" Savaul demanded as his jaw fell open. "Is the baby part Human?"

"That's not what happened," Prince Avalask assured him, but Savaul turned and shouldered the door open before he could say any more.

"The Humans did this to you?" Savaul demanded as he ran to Glidria's side and looked her over in horror.

Glidria gave him her best laugh in return and assured him, "It's alright, Savaul. It was a Human I quite liked."

But Savaul wasn't having it. He turned back to Prince Avalask and asked, "Can't you take it out of her?"

"Not safely."

"Safe for who?" Savaul repeated in overwhelm. "I don't care if it lives. I only want her to live."

"Savaul," Glidria scolded. "Women have been giving birth for centuries without the help of an Epic. I'll be fine."

Prince Avalask didn't even know how she was hiding such

78

excruciating pain. She lied as well as the Zhauri.

"It's going to be half-Human," Savaul exclaimed in disgust. "What are we supposed to do with a half-breed?"

Glidria reached to grab his hand and said, "We'll love him, Savaul. We'll teach him, and raise him, and maybe he'll help us end our war with Humanity someday."

That was another thing. The baby was going to be a boy. Prince Avalask had checked and told her so, wanting her to know, in case she didn't get to meet him.

"Only if you want it to end in our defeat," Savaul exclaimed. "He'll be a monster like the rest of them!"

"No, he will be whatever we raise him to be."

Savaul fell silent in shock as Gataan looked her over in silence and finally said, "It's going to kill you."

"It's the curse," Savaul said in despair. "It's using a Human baby to kill you from the inside out. Don't you see it?"

"Savaul," she said gruffly, "I need to know that if anything were to happen to me, that you'd honor my memory by ruling over Escalis the right way someday, in my place." He narrowed his eyes as Glidria said, "This war can be ended, but not if you try to end it by killing every last Human. That's how you'll destroy all of us."

Savaul had a tear in his eye as he growled, "If this kills you, then I promise to avenge you. It's a Human curse and a Human baby. They've taken everything from us, and we'll never forget it." Gataan nodded his agreement.

"That's not what I want from you," she growled back to him. "Do better, Savaul. *Be* better than your enemies, or you have nothing worth fighting for." She reached to stroke his hair as she said, "You're such a talented artist, and that's what you should embrace. Be a creator, not a destroyer. Find a way to make the world better, not just make it yours."

Glidria's entire body contracted in pain as Savaul's eyes grew

79

wide in despair.

"I need to talk to Fallistra," she said as Fallistra came to stand at Savaul's side. "Alone."

Prince Avalask opened his mouth to say, "I'll stay—"

"Give me a moment alone with my daughter," she insisted. "I need to speak with her. Go make the three of you some tea, and then come back. I'll be fine."

FALLISTRA

CHAPTER NINE

lidria had told her daughter the truth — that this was the end for her — and she shared as many sentiments of love and advice as she could before sharing instructions as well. A healthy baby boy was born shortly after, and in the chaos of healers scrambling about, trying to keep Glidria alive, Fallistra and the tiny baby in her arms were almost completely forgotten. Nobody noticed as she slipped into a side room and opened the window.

A cold wind cut through Fallistra's thick cloak and just about froze her uncovered fingers where she gripped the window ledge from the outside. She'd lowered herself as far as she could and dangled for only a moment before letting go and falling to the ground below, the lengths of several people between her and the frozen dirt.

She grunted as her knees buckled upon impact and she hit the ground hard, but she was on her feet and moving again in seconds. The precious baby in her arms stayed quiet as she readjusted the blankets around him to make sure the wind wasn't cutting through him too, and she moved quickly down the cobblestone path beneath a sky full of stars.

A full moon lit the buildings and walls around the city, and Fallistra pulled her scarf up to cover where the moonlight illuminated the golden tones of her hair — her most recognizable feature. She didn't want anyone to recognize her as she hurried through Treldinsae toward the outer gates.

The Escalis guarding the gates seemed mildly curious to know why a young woman was leaving the city with a baby in the middle of the night, but they let her pass without realizing who was in their midst.

A hint of powdered snow dusted the looming pines around her as she hurried through the surrounding homes and set her sights on heading south. She couldn't stop and ask for help — every single Escali in Treldinsae would happily render assistance, but she wanted to make sure she wouldn't be followed. There would be only one person left she couldn't elude. Prince Avalask would be able to find her no matter where she went, and she didn't know what he would want to do with the baby once he caught up to her.

"Fallistra?"

She'd just reached the trees when his voice came from behind her, and she slowed to a reluctant stop. Fallistra hugged her little brother to her chest and closed her eyes to gather her strength before she turned slowly around.

"Don't come any closer," she warned Prince Avalask, and he gave her a hint of a smile in return.

"Or what?"

"Or..." she had absolutely nothing to threaten or bargain with. "I would just prefer that you stay back for a moment."

The baby started to whimper in her arms and Fallistra tried to stroke his face and gently shush him, though it did nothing.

"Fallistra—"

"Is she gone?" she asked. Prince Avalask let a long, despairing breath escape before he nodded.

Fallistra swallowed hard, but she didn't have time to collapse and let her emotions overwhelm her.

"You didn't have to climb out the window," he said gently, and

Fallistra shrugged with mild embarrassment.

"I wanted you to be able to focus fully on trying to help Mother, and not have to worry about protecting the baby from everyone who wants him dead."

Fallistra didn't think Savaul would actually have it in him to kill a baby, but Gataan might, knowing that it had killed his sister. Gramsaf most certainly could if Savaul and Gataan had gone to get him.

"And… Mother and I talked about my best hope for escaping the curse," Fallistra said. "I have to get away from the rest of you. It's killing the women to punish the rest of you, but if we have no more ties, it's not really a punishment to you anymore. You won't be able to mourn if we don't have any more contact."

"So you're running away?" Prince Avalask asked, taking a step closer as Fallistra tried to hold the stirring baby back from her uncle.

"It's the only option that I think may work."

"And…" he raised his brows to clarify, "you're planning to take a newborn baby with you into the wilderness?"

Fallistra released a long exhale and admitted, "I don't have it perfectly planned out." He watched her with a pitying gaze as the baby started to fuss and squirm against his swaddling. "I know it will be difficult, but I can raise him away from everyone else. I *want* to. Mother's gone, and he's all that remains…"

Her breath finally caught in her throat, now that those words were spoken. Mother was gone. Never to laugh again, or teach Fallistra another word of the Human language in secret, never to meet the son she'd died for, never to rule the Escalis with her abrasive wisdom.

And tears sprang into her eyes as the baby in her arms started to wail, and her devastation crashed through her at the same time. It was all she could do to keep from sobbing along with him.

Prince Avalask stepped closer and said, "I'm sorry, Fallistra. I did everything I could to help her."

He meant to console her, but she stepped warily back as the baby screamed even louder. Fallistra had no idea how to comfort him. He was probably hungry, and she had nothing to give. What was she going to do?

"May I?" Prince Avalask asked, reaching for her to hand him over. "I won't hurt him."

She shook her head quickly.

"Your mother wanted to name him Architer. Archie for short, so it sounds both Human and Escali."

"I know that," she said, reaching her shoulder up to brush the tears from her eyes. "I... didn't want to start calling him by his name if you were just going to come destroy him. I know that's what the rest of the family wants..."

Prince Avalask's shoulders sank. "That's not what I'm here for." He reached for the writhing baby again, and repeated, "I promise, I won't hurt him."

Fallistra felt like she was being crushed, and like she was offering up her own beating heart as she finally held the shrieking infant out for Prince Avalask. But he took the baby gently, and little Archie fell silent as he looked up to Prince Avalask in wide eyed wonder. The Epic smiled and offered up his free hand, and Archie lunged to bite his knuckles. He sank his gums into Prince Avalask, and then he finally settled down to look curiously around.

Fallistra leaned in and rubbed at her cheeks one more time as the baby met her gaze, and she saw his eyes were deep, gemstone blue. "I thought he would have green eyes," she said, taking a deep breath, "like the rest of us."

Prince Avalask looked back up to her with concern and sympathy. "Fallistra... All babies have blue eyes."

"What?" Fallistra frowned, but saw that he was serious, and

84

knew this was just a taste of how much she didn't know.

"What am I going to do?" she asked softly. "I want to help him. I want to take him with me and raise him away from his father..."

"Away from his father?" Prince Avalask repeated, tilting his head with interest.

"Yes," she said with a long hesitation following. "I don't know how to say this, but... in the time Mother and I stayed with the Zhauri, I got to know them. And there's something about Maverick in particular that's unnerving. I know he loved Mother, but I've never been so unsettled by someone before."

Prince Avalask watched her for a long moment and asked, "What is it that worries you?"

"He doesn't feel empathy," she said. "He didn't care who he tortured or how he hurt them — all that ever mattered was his end goal. He'll kill people, and it won't rest on his conscience for a second. He had some sort of attachment to Mother — I do think he really cared for her — but I don't want my baby brother to grow up and be like him. I don't even want to give him the chance to meet his father."

Prince Avalask raised his eyebrows and said, "Half the blood in that baby's veins is Maverick's. We can keep him from his father, but... they'll always be connected."

"Archie won't be like him," Fallistra promised. "He'll be like us."

Fallistra reached a finger to baby Archie's tiny little hand, and he wrapped his fingers tightly around her as he squirmed again, and then cooed happily.

"Prince Avalask... I have to leave anyway. I can't stay with our family while this curse plagues us. Leaving is my best hope of survival. And I can take him with me."

Prince Avalask sighed heavily.

"Please. Let me take care of him."

"Alright," he conceded, looking back up to her. "I'll help you get set up. But… It's probably best if I don't see you often either, at least until we find a way to break the curse."

"I don't want anyone to be able to find us," she said. "Take us somewhere remote, where we can hunt, and tend our own little garden. And… fruit trees," she said as he gave her a sad smile.

"I will get you lots of fruit trees," he said, reaching for her hand. "Come on. Let's get you out of the cold, find a stand-in mother for Archie's first few months, and then we'll get you set up."

"Thank you," she whispered.

"You're welcome. Anything you ever need, Fallistra, I'll help you. Now let's go get warm."

PRINCE AVALASK

CHAPTER TEN

Prince Avalask set Fallistra up with a couple of the Escalis he'd known since childhood, who'd been in love since they were kids and had just had a daughter of their own. They'd take care of Fallistra and the baby — Archie — and so Prince Avalask set off to tell Maverick.

He found Maverick and Hakkrui bolting out of the Dragona in pursuit of something as their white cloaks billowed behind them. Prince Avalask leapt and reappeared far enough in front of them that they could skid to a quick stop without barreling into him.

"We're on our way to get it," Hakkrui said quickly, glancing to Maverick beside him. "We'll get there faster if you take us."

Maverick's jaw fell open as he saw Prince Avalask's face, and he whispered, "She's already dead."

Prince Avalask nodded bitterly in return and replied, "She's gone."

"And the baby? Did it live?"

Prince Avalask would have lied to him if he had any chance of getting away with it, but Maverick was far too good at reading him. "Yes," Prince Avalask said truthfully. "The baby made it. Fallistra has it now."

Maverick held both hands to his head in anguish, but he also let a sigh of relief escape that at least one thing hadn't ended in tragedy. "Where is Fallistra?"

"Still in danger until that curse is broken," Prince Avalask replied. "Where is it?"

"We're on our way to get it," Maverick said. "Avery hid it, but we got the location."

Prince Avalask felt a frown come to his face as he asked, "How did you find it?"

"By doing things the smart way, Avalask. While you were trying to catch Avery himself, we dug into his history and found out who and what to threaten, to get him to come to us. He told us where to go. Navvad's keeping an eye on him until we get back with the curse."

Prince Avalask didn't know what Avery had left to threaten with his parents both dead now. He had a couple friends at the Dragona, Anna, a couple other mages he trained with... a couple girls in his hometown of Keldrosa he always went back to visit... But nothing that would have convinced the Epic to give up the curse. Prince Avalask didn't know who or what the Zhauri had found to threaten.

"Let's go then. I'll take you," Prince Avalask said, holding a hand out to both of them. He put the strongest shield around his thoughts that he could possibly muster, but Maverick sensed his underlying intents anyway.

"I want to see the baby first," Maverick replied.

"Help me destroy the curse, and then we'll talk," Prince Avalask replied.

Maverick watched him for a long, calculating moment, then whispered, "You've already made up your mind."

"Fallistra wants to keep and raise the baby," Prince Avalask said. "She'll take good care of it."

"That's fine. Our work isn't great for raising kids anyway," Maverick said with a gesture to himself and Hakkrui. "I'm not trying to steal it and run away, I just want to meet my own child. You haven't even told me if it's a boy or girl."

"There's not much point telling you a gender when you aren't going to get to meet it," Prince Avalask replied, seeing fury fill Maverick's eyes. "Fallistra wants to raise the baby alone, away from the influence of the Zhauri, and I'm in full support of her decision."

"You can't keep my own child from me," Maverick replied in a dangerous whisper.

"Maybe when it gets older, we could —"

"Do not think that I'll stand here and accept whatever menial terms you're willing to give me," Maverick hissed in return. "Have you forgotten who you're talking to?"

"I haven't," Prince Avalask replied fearlessly. "And it's your reputation for terror that has me standing here, telling you no."

"And how about that curse, Prince Avalask?" Maverick asked in a cool rage. "You give me that baby, or I'll keep it intact. The curse will be the least of your worries after you decide you're going to try to keep my newborn from me."

Prince Avalask stared hard at him — it would be so easy to just let him meet Archie. The little boy could grow up with his sister's guidance, and only spend winters with his father.

But Fallistra had seen the same frightening depth to Maverick that Prince Avalask had. The man lived with the intent to conquer, to rule everything beneath him. Archie was more than a child to love — he was an asset Maverick wanted. A powerful heir, and an incredible weapon if the Zhauri had any sway over his life. Prince Avalask couldn't watch Maverick taint his sister's son.

"Fallistra may not live long enough to raise that baby if the curse remains," Maverick warned. Prince Avalask already knew that was the case, and happened to have the two Zhauri in front of him who knew where to find it. And he found himself wondering if he could get the location out of them too.

Maverick threw his head back and released a deep, unsettling laugh as he sensed the intention Prince Avalask was pondering. "You don't know the first thing about working a victim for information," Maverick told him. "And that's a line you can never uncross. You're too softhearted for this life, Avalask. Do yourself a favor and stick with your moral high ground. You'll feel a lot better about yourself."

Hakkrui glanced to Maverick and chuckled as he said, "We'd also be the wrong people to start with, if this is the path you really want to take. You won't get anything out of us, and you'll bring the wrath of the Zhauri down in return. You'll gain nothing, and it will cost you everything."

"I've seen you do this," Prince Avalask replied through a darkening glare, "in your card game with Fallistra. She had the hand to beat you, and you gave her such doubt in her ability to win, that she surrendered it." Hakkrui folded his arms as Prince Avalask said, "You won't have the same luck with me. I *know* I hold the cards to beat you. There is not a thing either of you could do to stop me if I decided to pry the curse's location from your lips right now."

Maverick raised his eyebrows, not looking the least bit frightened. "If only this were a game of cards…" he mused, looking as confident as Hakkrui when he'd intimidated Fallistra out of her win. "It would be your move, Avalask."

Prince Avalask looked them both over once more, and the question popped into his mind…

Why not just give them Archie?

If he was willing to stoop to all their terrible lows, there remained no reason to keep Archie from them.

They'd all be the same.

And he decided he liked his moral high ground. He wanted to remain the Epic who was above torture. Who did things the right way. Because it was a bunch of little concessions like this that led to becoming his father.

"I'm leaving," Prince Avalask told them both. "Not because I am afraid of you. Because I am better than your lows, and that's why we're keeping Glidria's baby. I'd like it to be as soft hearted as I am."

"If it's a girl, the curse might kill it anyway," Maverick warned him as he turned to leave. "You'd rather put Glidria's children in danger than let me have any influence in their lives?"

"Don't turn this around on me," Prince Avalask snapped back. "You're the one keeping the curse intact. You're the one who would rather see them killed than raised away from you."

"I'll find that baby," Maverick hissed as Prince Avalask rolled his eyes.

"I wish you the best of luck," he replied, and Maverick lunged in a vain attempt to grab him right before the Epic danced easily back.

"AVALASK!" he roared, his calm finally shattering as Prince Avalask waved a few fingers in farewell and vanished.

Prince Avalask landed in the Epic's Hall in Dekaron — a long, elegant chamber with a throne-like chair at the end. He and Gramsaf used to take turns down here, sitting and listening to the requests of the people. Escalis came to King Izfazara with their complaints, and to the Epics with their requests and needs, and Prince Avalask generally enjoyed being able to help those who came to him.

He lowered himself into the uncomfortable throne of a chair, and finally let the events of the day wash over him as he released a deep breath. He always found himself composed while he had tasks to attend to and immediate goals to accomplish. It was always in the silence afterward that he was finally able to comprehend and process the distress of the day.

There was never free time, but every once in a while, there *was* silence.

And Glidria was dead.

They would never rule together as the queen and her Epic.

His hopes of seeing his sister end the Human Escali war would never come to pass. He'd have to hand the crown to Savaul, who was already more like their father than Prince Avalask wanted to acknowledge. Now that Glidria was gone, Gramsaf's hatred for the Humans would taint any chance of Savaul ever wanting anything more than to kill them.

Fallistra was in hiding, unable to even come visit.

The curse would continue to plague them, making it so nobody in the royal family could marry without their new wife being immediately killed in a freak accident or illness.

Prince Avalask hadn't even managed to keep the dream alive that he and Avery might not live their entire lives as combatants.

The world would go on exactly as it always had, and nothing he'd hoped to accomplish mattered.

Prince Avalask found himself wandering to the chambers where their translation program was housed. There were other things he could be doing — such as trying to get to Savaul and Gataan before Gramsaf turned them into himself with hatred. He could be accompanying Glidria's body to the site where they'd burn it. Or he could check in on Fallistra to make sure she was settling in comfortably.

But instead, he pushed open the door to where his class lived.

They heard the door opening, and he sank into a chair as Sass poked her head around the corner. "Prince Avalask, if you don't come visit us more often, we're going to fire you from being our captor."

"Knock it off," Flora admonished as she came up behind Sass

and saw Prince Avalask's sullen face. "Something's wrong."

"What's happened?" Sass asked, lifting one leg over the back of her chair to seat herself with a bouncy enthusiasm.

"Are you alright?" Flora asked, sitting beside Sass as Darin came to the doorway to stand with folded arms.

Prince Avalask opened his mouth, but didn't know where to start. The ongoing curse, the Zhauri, and the unending Epic feud? The death of his grandmother? Aunt Ildra? Queen Nori? His Mother? Glidria? Fallistra and the baby never being able to come home?

The death of every positive future he'd ever envisioned?

An exhale of a sob was all that came out of his mouth, and he leaned to fold his arms across the desk and lay his face down as Sass and Flora both jumped out of their chairs to come comfort him.

INTERLUDE

FOUR YEARS LATER

CHAPTER ELEVEN

rince Avalask had an absolute monster in his hands as he leapt across the continent, and the young girl kicked and screamed and tried to bite him.

"Take me back!" she snarled as she writhed and dug her nails into his arm.

"I am trying to help you!" he exclaimed as he made the final leap and landed outside the door to Fallistra's cabin.

The girl, Allie, was just about demented. Her screams echoed through the whole forest as she tried to punch and kick in a scramble to do as much damage as she could. She was just a child though — her worst wasn't all that bad.

Just as he thought it, Allie managed to rake her nails painfully down his arm, leaving five giant welts behind as he exclaimed, "I'm not holding you anymore! You're the one who won't get off!"

He was attempting to set her down gently, without throwing her into the cabin wall or out into the field. But now she'd switched tactics and was trying to strangle the Epic as he grabbed her by the wrists and pried her grasp away.

"What is going on?" Fallistra exclaimed from the doorway. She dashed forward to help pull the terror off Prince Avalask as she called back to Archie, "Stay in the house!"

97

Allie scratched and spat at both of them, shrieking again as Fallistra tried to help set her down. Allie flailed to one side and got her teeth into Fallistra, which was when Archie bolted out to help. He had enough momentum when he collided with her that he was able to wrench her off and throw her straight off their little porch. Exactly what Prince Avalask had been trying *not* to do.

Allie crashed into the grass and scrambled back to her feet, hissing at the three of them before she turned and bolted into the trees.

"What was that?!" Archie exclaimed, watching in shock as the girl ran off. He was just about her same age — both of them kids by Human and Escali standards.

"You wanted more Tallies to befriend," Prince Avalask replied, unable to resist laughing at the look of horror on Archie's face. "I just found you another one — Human mother, and one *idiot* of an Escali father."

"What's wrong with her?" Archie whispered, unable to believe that the monster he'd just seen was one of his own kind.

"It's a long story, but I don't think she's ever seen an Escali before today," Prince Avalask said. He looked to Fallistra and explained, "Her Escali father went all the way to Tekada to find her mother, and of course he got caught. She just watched him die, and saw her mother taken by the Tekadans. She is acting like a little demon, but... you can't really blame her, given what she just witnessed."

"That just happened... right now?" Archie asked in clear concern. He looked back out to the forest where she'd disappeared, and Prince Avalask sensed he wanted to help.

"This is where she went," Prince Avalask said, projecting a tiny recreation of the forest onto the ground before them. He lit a small section in red to show where Allie had stopped to rip up a bunch of plants and kick every tree — her own violent way to grieve and rage.

Archie looked up and asked, "Does she even know she's half Escali?"

"If she didn't already, she does now," Prince Avalask replied as Archie looked back to the forest again. And without asking anybody for permission, he took off into the trees after her.

"Be careful," Fallistra called after him, and the Epic could feel she was debating whether to follow or let him go alone.

Fallistra looked more like Glidria than ever, and as they watched Archie disappear into the forest, Prince Avalask had to remind himself he wasn't standing next to his sister. Just her grown-up, golden-haired, opinionated daughter.

"You got a few minutes to catch up?" he asked.

"Always," she replied, gesturing for him to join her inside. He occasionally came to visit, but usually just spent time with Archie, telling him stories and bringing new things the kid had never seen. They always called it their *boy time,* which was really a clever way for him to not see too much of Fallistra. "Perhaps you could start by explaining why you just showed up on my doorstep with a demon in your arms?"

He exhaled his amusement in return. "I don't have many places for hiding a half-Human," he replied, seating himself at their small table as Fallistra moved to heat water for tea without asking if he wanted any or not. "I was hoping you could look after her. It might be nice for Archie to have a friend he can see more than a few times a year."

"There is the curse to consider," Fallistra reminded him. "If Archie makes the mistake of loving her, it could cost that girl her life."

"Fallistra, if it hasn't killed you yet, then you're right about there being loopholes. Maybe the curse won't affect him at all, with that Human blood in his veins."

"No, I think it's waiting until he's older," Fallistra countered. "Abernathy wanted the *men* of our family to suffer the loss he felt. I don't think he had children in mind when he cast it."

"If you're right, it could just be a matter of a few years until the curse targets you next. You'll need to separate yourself from Archie before the curse decides to consider him a man like the rest of us."

Fallistra waved that thought away and replied, "If it's going to kill me, then it'll kill me. I'm not going to abandon Archie in an attempt to stave it off."

Prince Avalask gave her an accepting shrug and said, "It's up to you. You can always call for me if you think it's starting to target you, but… That's also when it's too late for me to do anything."

"How are Savaul and Gataan?" Fallistra asked suddenly, but he knew the question was just to step away from thoughts of the curse.

"Mean and spiteful, just like their father," Prince Avalask replied with a wry smile. "I'm telling you, Fallistra, I need to find a way to make sure Izfazara lives forever, because Savaul will burn this world down in the name of vengeance if he takes the crown."

"It's still your choice who gets it," Fallistra replied thoughtfully.

"And my choices are Savaul, Gataan, and Gramsaf," Prince Avalask said with a short sigh. "Unless you're insinuating I should be considering you…" He wasn't sure why the thought had never crossed his mind. Would the Escalis accept Fallistra? They'd *loved* Glidria. They could love her daughter.

"Not me," she said, nodding out to the trees, where Archie had run after the wreck of a girl he wanted to help. "Have you thought about it?"

He laughed and said, "I appreciate your optimism, but I would be flayed alive if I even suggested it. The Escalis will never be ready for a half-Human to rule over them, regardless of who he is, or how good he could be."

"They could be upset for the next hundred years. It doesn't

change the fact that the choice is yours. And it seems a better outcome than Savaul — how did you put it? — *burning the world down?"*

Prince Avalask shook his head and looked out to where Archie had caught up with Allie. She'd grabbed a large stick and was advancing on him as he backed slowly away.

His hair glinted gold wherever the dappled sunlight struck it, and Prince Avalask said aloud, "He does look incredibly like you and your mother." He watched over the distance as Archie tried to look unthreatening, holding his hands out and open. Allie butted the end of her stick straight into his chest and knocked him back a few steps as he gasped in surprise.

"He looks even more like his father," Fallistra replied. "It's unnerving sometimes, but he's a good kid. There are only a few times I ever see real hints of Maverick in him. Usually when he wants something."

Prince Avalask found himself amused as he watched Archie glance nervously around the empty forest, as though he couldn't believe he'd actually put himself in a situation alone with the monster girl.

"I'm going to murder you, gut you out, and then boil your liver inside your skull for dinner," Allie snarled, still holding the large stick in her hands to warn him back.

"That sounds like a *lot* of effort," Archie replied, keeping his wits about him as she hissed furiously at his attempt to defuse the situation. Prince Avalask would have laughed if they weren't both so afraid.

Allie was all threats and hot air — the way any young Escali would have reacted to a frightening situation. Prince Avalask would have sworn she *was* a full blooded Escali if not for her flattened teeth and the clarity in her brown eyes. She must have broken her arm-spikes off to fit in on Tekada too, because Archie

101

had them and she didn't.

"Who are you?" she demanded, taking another threatening step forward as Archie maintained his distance this time to avoid being struck. "And what do you want?"

Archie met her eyes, and with a heart full of sincerity, he whispered, "*I'm like you*. I don't want anything—"

"If I'd wanted such a useless answer, I would have gone and caught a forest frog and asked him!" She lunged and swung at him again as he darted back from her strike. "Tell me who you are and what you want!"

Prince Avalask smirked to himself as Fallistra returned to the table and poured him a cup of northern tea. It was her favorite, and he'd always made sure they had a constant supply of the dried leaves to keep them comfortable.

"What are Savaul and Gataan doing about the curse?" she asked as she seated herself and blew steam from the surface of her own tea.

"The three of us all decided to never marry," Prince Avalask replied. "Bonding is so powerful, and none of us want to go through it just to lose our mates right after."

"So... no more kids for the royal family?"

"At least until we find a way to break the curse," Prince Avalask replied. "You're the same age as Savaul and Gataan. There's no reason you couldn't marry. You're all of age this year, and the curse shouldn't care, since you'd be with someone outside the family."

"I think I'd rather wait until it's broken as well, since none of us know exactly what triggers it," Fallistra said, rubbing at her hairline in distress. "This is all so unfortunate. You'd be such a good father. It isn't fair none of us can have what we want in life, all because of shanking Abernathy."

"For what it's worth, I was always hesitant about having kids," he said with an uncomfortable shrug of acceptance. "A part of me is relieved I'll never have to put my own son through the Epic's existence. We all eventually follow the same path, from extreme power and reverence to inevitable bitterness."

"You don't seem bitter to me. Maybe you'll be the exception."

"I'd be the first. Avery is already there – or, *Sir Avery*, I should say. He went and got himself a fun little title, in case anybody *didn't* already know he was important." Fallistra breathed a mild chuckle at the mockery in his tone. Prince Avalask leaned to take a sip of the tea in his hands, and he looked back up to Fallistra as he tasted the spicy warmth. "This is really good. What did you put in it?"

"A secret, addictive ingredient to make sure you stay here and tell me everything going on back home," she said as he raised his eyebrows in amusement. "Most just call it cinnamon."

He smiled and took another sip before settling in to tell her everything going on with the remaining, entirely male, royal family. Mostly he told her how aggressive they'd all become toward Humans, with the exception of their ever-fair-minded king, who didn't want to escalate their war against Humanity if he could avoid it.

"I wish I could come see Savaul without triggering the curse," Fallistra lamented, gazing toward the fireplace in a moment of sadness. "I've missed our scheming, and I'm sure I could talk him down from at least some of his hostility."

"I don't know that it would be a good idea."

"Of course it's not," Fallistra grumbled. "It would be a death sentence. Savaul and I were too close. I won't be able to see him until the day the curse is broken."

Prince Avalask could stop in at Fallistra's cabin, chat like acquaintances for ten minutes, then go the next six months without seeing her or thinking of her all too often. It was just enough non-contact that the curse didn't seem to have interest in targeting her for the sake of hurting Prince Avalask.

But Savaul was different. It was best that he knew nothing of her existence or wellbeing, otherwise the curse would have an easy opportunity to harm him by killing her. He couldn't distance himself from loving her, which was why Fallistra asked Prince Avalask to never bring him along. It pained her too, but it was her only option.

"I *have* tried to stop him," Prince Avalask admitted, "but Savaul keeps going behind my back and assembling elite teams to track you down and bring you home. I'm sure he's gotten one or two past my notice by now. Of course, I've told him how dangerous the curse would be to you if you ever returned, but..."

Prince Avalask paused as Fallistra broke into a mischievous grin. He'd expected his news to be distressing, but she just looked to her uncle in amusement and said, "You tell Savaul I welcome his challenge." Prince Avalask couldn't contain his surprise as she explained, "We used to play hiders and finders across all of Dekaron, and Savaul never once beat me. You tell him *Game On* from me, just as long as he knows Archie isn't part of the game. Anything happens to that kid, and I'll end Savaul's hopes of ever becoming king. Very slowly and painfully."

Prince Avalask let an amused exhale escape, and said, "I'll pass the word along."

The front door creaked open, and Archie slid quietly into the cabin as though hoping nobody would notice him.

"Archie? Is that a black eye?" Fallistra asked, rising from her chair as Archie turned away and tried to hide it. He slunk back to a wooden chest and pulled it open to pull a whole armful of blankets out. "Let your uncle take a look at it. He can fix it up in a few seconds."

"Then she'll just give me another one," Archie replied with a frown, closing the chest lid as he retreated into the room where they slept at night. He returned with every blanket off his bed and then moved back to the door, as though he was about to escape without any further explanation.

"Archie," Fallistra stopped him. "What are you doing?"

"She's not going to come in," Archie replied, holding up the armful of blankets. "And I don't want her to freeze to death. It gets cold at night."

"Are you planning to stay out there too?" Prince Avalask asked as his nephew nodded.

"She's from Tekada," he said. "She doesn't know the first thing about the forest."

"I honestly don't think there's a bear or tama cat out there that will dare to mess with her," Prince Avalask replied with an easy smile.

"She may not know that. I don't want her to be afraid all night."

Prince Avalask did really like this kid, and Fallistra was right. He was the same giving, protective type his mother had always been.

Fallistra sighed and said, "Don't leave without some food and tea to bring with you. Maybe she'll see it as a peace offering and not blacken your second eye." She gave Prince Avalask an amused smirk as she moved to pour tea into a reed cannister and seal it beneath a wax-wedge lid. She wrapped up a few apples and cheese crumbles, and put them in a bag to hand Archie before he left. "Tell her all about the warm fire we've got in here, and that she's welcome to it whenever she's ready."

"I will," Archie said very seriously before Fallistra kissed him on the head and he left with a face full of importance, and duty, and what was going to be some serious self-sacrifice if he was going to stay out in the cold to keep her company. He was a kid on a mission.

Archie left, and Fallistra came back to top off Prince Avalask's cooling tea as he looked up to her and asked, "Are you sure you don't want any kids of your own? You are good at this."

105

"Thanks, Avalask, but two is already more than I signed up for. It might be different if you'd shown up on my doorstep with a sweet little girl who wanted to help me with the sewing. I'm pretty sure the one you're dropping off will keep me busy enough that I won't miss having my own."

He laughed in return and she sat across from him with her own grin.

"How long do you guess it'll take before Archie convinces her to come inside?"

"It's hard to say," Fallistra said, blowing softly across her tea as she looked to the crackling fire in thought. "Girl seems like she'll be pretty stubborn, but Archie's got a certain... convincing charm to him. There are times he'll say something that sounds so Zhauri, a part of me worries that Maverick has been here to meet him in secret." She took another sip and added, "He can be persuasive when he wants to be."

Prince Avalask looked thoughtfully to the fire as well. "A part of me is surprised Maverick hasn't been here yet."

"I think we should just consider ourselves grateful," Fallistra replied. "For whatever reason, he's decided to leave us alone. I'm sure it won't stay this way forever."

"No, it won't," Prince Avalask agreed. "All we can do is prepare Archie to be better than his father, and try to keep Maverick away as long as possible. And we'll hope that's enough."

"I'd like you to start integrating him into the Escali world," Fallistra said as Prince Avalask tapped absentmindedly at the side of his teacup. "I know it won't be easy, but... if you tell the Escalis to accept him, that he's half Human but he's on our side, I'm sure they'll at least try to tolerate him."

"That could prove tricky," Prince Avalask said. "Savaul, Gataan, and Gramsaf won't have it."

"Izfazara will see his value," Fallistra said. "Just make sure you

106

get Izfazara' s support first. If the two of you speak well of Archie, the Escalis may even come to like him. He's smart, and courageous, and he's a good kid. If the Escalis can accept him, he might be able to help us really change things with the Humans."

Prince Avalask nodded and said, "Alright, I'll bring him to meet Izfazara and see where we can go from there. But I am *not* taking Allie with me," he said as Fallistra broke into a light laugh as well. "She'll have to stay here with you while I'm introducing Archie to the family."

"That's fine by me. I'm sure we'll be here practicing our braiding while you're away."

"Yeah, good luck with that."

"And good luck with the rest of our family. I'm sure they'll just love him."

PART TWO

SIX YEARS LATER

PART TWO

SIX YEARS LATER

Prince Avalask

Chapter Twelve

Prince Avalask was on an absolute fool's mission, stalking invisibly through the Human streets of Keldrosa. He was looking for boys throughout the city who seemed to be able to use magic, and actively cursed that this was the mission the rest of his family thought needed to take priority over all else. There was an elderly couple in Zinta he'd much rather be assisting, or a tiny baby who'd been born early in Drukmir, who might not live without the help of magic. People cried out for him across the continent at all times, and rather than aid any of them, he was on the hunt for little Human boys so he could steal one.

And yes, he knew how *not valiant* that sounded.

All of this was based on a rumor — *a rumor* — that Rallek had brought back to Dekaron four years ago. Rallek had turned out to be one of the best informants in the whole Escali Translation Program the minute he graduated, and he'd heard talk among the Humans that Sir Avery had borne a son in secret. No other information, nothing even close to a real shred of evidence — just a rumor.

But Savaul had made the investigation of that rumor his personal purpose in life. And the one shred of evidence Savaul could manage to conjure was that whenever the Escalis would come close to Keldrosa, Sir Avery would arrive to defend it. Without fail, no matter where else the Escalis would attack, Keldrosa always received his utmost attention.

Even Izfazara thought Savaul might be onto something, and Prince Avalask had no choice once the king had made his opinion known. Prince Avalask was to scout around the entire city, spot any boy he thought might potentially be Sir Avery's son, and then he'd watch all of them as the Escalis attacked the city. He'd see if Avery was truly there to protect his firstborn, or if he had something else of value hidden among the thriving metropolis.

Prince Avalask had found a handful of kids throughout the day who were sort of close, but none quite fit what he was looking for. There was an older boy, Dauer, who lived in an expensive mansion outside the city and seemed to emanate the most power of anyone he'd found. But he was closer to eleven or twelve, in their slow-aging Human years. Prince Avalask found two boys with magic, closer to the four-year-old he was looking for, but their powers were weak by comparison. And he didn't spot either of them using more than one.

Even if this kid really was in Keldrosa, it was highly likely his powers weren't even beginning to show up yet. In which case, Prince Avalask would have to rely solely on spotting where Avery landed and who he checked on first.

Evening came, and he shaded the entire area so no mages could sense the Escali attackers approaching.

Their raiding party was small — less than fifty — and as soon as true darkness descended, they melted into the city and began to light fires.

Alarm bells rang, and city guardsmen ran out to face their attackers, but were quickly cut down by the Escalis' superior speed and strength.

Avery arrived within seconds of the bells ringing, and Prince

Avalask focused on nothing else. He only had attention for Sir Avery as the Human Epic bolted into the fight and lashed back at the attacking Escalis, killing a handful before Prince Avalask appeared and leapt into the fray.

They ended up in the sky almost immediately. Sir Avery called a bolt of lightning from the heavens to strike Prince Avalask, and the Escali Epic reacted on immediate instinct to block the immensity of the sky's power. Prince Avalask had planned this part too though — he flashed Sir Avery a knowing grin and told him, "I hope you're not *missing anything* from the city below us."

Avery's eyes widened in disbelief, which was the moment Prince Avalask knew Savaul really had found something here. Was it actually a child? Or maybe a sweetheart he loved and wanted to protect?

The two snarled and fought, this time resembling more of the frenzy their fathers used to show in battle, but Sir Avery held his ground and never strayed far from the city. More mages jumped in and helped fight the Escalis off, and when there were finally enough magic users at the scene, the Escalis whistled to each other the sound for retreat.

Prince Avalask finally backed off, but he watched Sir Avery carefully to see where he might go. The Human Epic stayed in the city's central square and gave no indication of where Prince Avalask should be looking. There *was* something here. He just couldn't figure out who, or what, or where to look.

He stayed and watched closely until he finally spotted something out of place.

It was Allie — Archie's little monster friend who'd grown into an independent, fire-hearted rebel of a young woman — running from Keldrosa to get to the next city unseen. She wore a golden band around her wrist that kept Prince Avalask from sensing her, and he would have missed her entirely if he hadn't spotted her with his good old-fashioned eyeballs.

He split his attention to watch both her and Sir Avery, but Avery wasn't about to give anything away, and Allie was clearly done with whatever she'd been doing in Keldrosa. He leapt out to her, and nearly startled the life out of her as she skidded to a stop in the fallen autumn leaves and whipped around to see him. Her tied back, waist-length blonde hair swung behind her with the sharp movement.

"What are you doing?" she demanded, taking a quick, guilty step back from him. "You shouldn't startle people like this!"

"I was just having a nice little wonder, about why you're sneaking out of Keldrosa with a shade band around your arm."

She glanced down at the golden circlet, then back up to Prince Avalask as she said, "I was just visiting a couple friends when the Escalis decided to attack the place. Not exactly somewhere I wanted to stick around."

But in her head, he could hear the loud, overpowering thought, *Don't think about it. He'll hear you. Don't think about anything remotely related.*

"Your thoughts have a different story to tell," he told her as she broke into a scowl.

"You know I hate when you read my mind."

"I do," he agreed, adjusting his cloak so he could seat himself on a fallen log and watch her with amusement, "but neither of us are leaving this hillside until you tell me exactly what you were doing in Keldrosa. You can tell me with your words, or let your thoughts do the talking."

Allie's scowl darkened as she snarled, "You can't keep me here."

"Oh, can't I?"

He waited patiently, and just listened as she sneered at him and looked around the tall cedars for ideas. A small brook gurgled not far off, on its way down the hill and into the nearest valley. The

114

forest was full of sticks, and small creatures in hiding, but there was nothing she could use against him.

He felt her thinking through her options as she briefly considered taking the shade band off her wrist, throwing it as far from herself as she could get it, and then calling to Sir Avery for help. While that was the one tactic that may have actually worked, it also gave away who she'd come to Keldrosa to assist.

"I thought you might have been here to give Sir Avery a hand," Prince Avalask said, taking amusement from the sneer she gave him in return. "So let me try to fill in the parts I'm unsure about, and we'll see what you think of my guesses. How's that sound?"

Allie made an attempt to turn and bolt away, but Prince Avalask's magic easily stopped her in her tracks. It was harmless, but infuriated the girl as she seethed, "It's wrong of you to hold me here."

"What I *think* happened," he said without much concern, "is that one of your Escali friends tipped you off about the attack, and said we were going after something of value to Sir Avery. And you went straight to Sir Avery and warned him."

Allie was trying as hard as she could to keep her thoughts locked in silence, but there was no way to shield them. She was too young to have the discipline the Zhauri wielded, to only think the thoughts she wanted him to hear. And he could tell so far, everything he'd said was exactly right.

"And after you'd warned him, I think he enlisted your help," Prince Avalask said, sensing again that his version of the story was ringing true. "He knew I'd track his every move from the moment he arrived in the city, so he put a shade band on you, and sent you in to protect his son. You grabbed the kid and got him out of the city before it was attacked."

Allie answered with a grin this time, "Sounds like you figured it all out, Prince Avalask. I'll promise you one thing though, with my

115

help, you'll never find his son."

He frowned in concentration, trying to read the riddle she'd just laid before him. It was both honest and deceitful. True, but somehow also misleading. He'd gotten something wrong, but she wasn't making it easy to determine what.

"It wasn't a child," Prince Avalask ventured, and she just raised her hands to either side to say she had no idea.

"You tell me. You're the one who's supposed to be so good at guessing."

"Or..." he mused, watching her closely, "it's not a boy." He raised his eyebrows as alarms went off in Allie's mind. "*Allie*. Sir Avery was hiding a *daughter* in Keldrosa?"

Allie huffed a deep growl of frustration as Prince Avalask asked, "Does she have her powers yet? How old is she?"

"Are you sure you don't want to just start listing off numbers and stop when you read you've hit the right one?" she snarled.

"I *will*," he said without shame, "but it seems a waste of time when you're right here to tell me."

"She's *four*," Allie replied in disdain. "And no, I don't think there are any powers yet. I don't even think she knows Sir Avery is her father," Allie added. "There wasn't a lot of time to ask questions with the Escalis on the brink of attacking."

"Where is she?" Prince Avalask asked.

"*That*, you won't get from me," Allie replied. "I handed her off to another couple. And while you're out here with me, I'm guessing Sir Avery's already retrieved her."

Prince Avalask looked quickly back to Keldrosa to find that Avery was gone. Shanking life, while he'd been distracted with Allie, the Epic had gotten away with her.

"Prince Avalask," Allie said slowly, now watching him with scrutiny. "Please tell me you're better than hunting down a *four-year-old* who's just learning to sing the alphabet. I know killing is a normal part of your every day, but—"

"I don't want to kill her," he replied. "I want to spare her from the life her father will pass down to her — that is, if girls can even inherit the Epic powers."

Allie gave him a different kind of scowl now and said, "Girls get powers the same way boys do. It's just been pure chance that all the Epics have been boys. A first-born daughter might not be what we're used to, but she'll be just as strong."

Prince Avalask put a hand to his forehead and said, "I need to go."

Without another word to the Tally on the hillside, he leapt away and reappeared in Dekaron, where Savaul, Gataan, Gramsaf, and Izfazara all waited.

"Well?" Savaul asked, his eyes full of eagerness and anticipation. "Was I right? Did you find him?"

"You were right," Prince Avalask conceded as Savaul's face lit with enthusiasm.

"Did you find him?"

"No," Prince Avalask said with a bitter shake of his head. "It turns out we all made a terrible oversight."

"What do you mean *we* made an oversight?" Gramsaf demanded. "You were supposed to be watching every boy in that city even close to the right age—"

"It's a girl," Prince Avalask cut him off. "I have it on good authority that Avery had a daughter, and I didn't even catch a glimpse of her."

Everybody's faces slackened in shock — not because she was a girl, but because she existed. A true, serious threat to all of them.

"How old?" Izfazara asked.

"Four years," Prince Avalask replied, feeling an anxious flutter in his chest as he took a deep breath and said, "I'll marry." Savaul's bright expression of triumph fell as the reality of the situation sank

117

in. "If we take a few months to find the right woman, then nine more until our next Epic is born, we'll only be five years behind the Human Epic. And since Escali childhoods are so much shorter, the two of them should come into their powers right around the same time."

"What if you have a girl too?" Savaul asked in horror. "Or what if the wife you take doesn't survive long enough to have the baby?" He looked to the rest of the family and said, "We could be ending the Epic bloodline if we let him marry while the curse still exists."

"Putting it off won't make it any less dangerous," Izfazara said. "The Zhauri hold the curse, and there's no force in the world strong enough to take it from their hands. If we don't take the risk now, we won't have an Epic to oppose the Human Epic. This... is unfortunate," Izfazara said with an apologetic look toward Prince Avalask, "but we have all thought long and hard about it, and none of us have been able to come up with any other choice."

"I wouldn't wish this upon my worst enemy," Gramsaf said, in a surprising tone of empathy. "To bond with somebody you know will have to die, is a fate crueler than any I know."

For being such a wretched father and living a life with almost no affection whatsoever, Gramsaf had taken the death of his wife extremely hard.

"What if nobody volunteers for the competitions?" Savaul asked. "We have to tell them the consequence of joining the family. They have to know what they're competing for."

"Of course we'll tell them," Izfazara said with a mild scowl. "I guarantee they'll line up anyway. Our strongest women will come from far and wide to compete for the honor of marrying into the family, even if it's just for long enough to give us the Epic heir."

Prince Avalask didn't want to believe they were really going to do this, but there wasn't another option. They *had* to have an Epic to oppose Avery's daughter, and Escalis couldn't have kids without marriage and bonding first. Falling in love was inevitable, and his new wife would die for it. The curse had officially killed every woman in the family — including Fallistra a couple years back.

Gramsaf gave a dark, humorless laugh and said, "You always thought I did such a terrible job raising you, Avalask. I can't wait to see how you do with your own son. You're creating a weapon — remember that. There's no room for coddling."

"I'm sure I'll figure it out," Prince Avalask replied, still determined to never become what he'd seen in his father.

"Just wait, you'll see," Gramsaf assured him with a look of knowing. "Suffering the loss of a mate will change you, Avalask. Then when your own son is half grown and thinks he knows everything, spouting off about how *Humanity's not so bad*, and *we should all just get along*, it'll drive you to the same anger it's driven me. Just you watch."

"I am not you," Prince Avalask said flatly, not allowing Gramsaf's words to permeate in the least.

"Not yet," Gramsaf agreed, "but after this, you will be."

PRINCE AVALASK

CHAPTER THIRTEEN

The competitions to marry the Epic were scheduled quickly, and Izfazara was right. Competitors lined up from across the whole continent for a chance to win and die for him.

The whole family agreed on one thing — Prince Avalask wasn't allowed to watch them compete. That was typically the tradition anyway, but it made even more sense now because he didn't want to meet his new wife early and possibly trigger the curse sooner than he had to.

Also... how upsetting would it be to fall in love with a competitor who didn't end up winning?

He was perfectly fine not watching as they narrowed several thousand contestants down to forty-eight by way of a multi-city obstacle run. He didn't mind missing the narrowing of the pool to twenty-four by arena-style mass combat. He was unbothered as he missed the two versus two matches, and the quarterfinal combat selections.

But he started to get antsy as the semifinals came and he still wasn't allowed to see the participants. All he had were Savaul's laughing assurances that he was almost certainly going to be marrying *an ox of a woman* named Dreya. And if Savaul was to be believed, she could break a man between her hands without a bead of sweat on her brow.

He found himself unable to sleep as Dreya and Ninkila made it into the final round.

"She's going to win," Savaul assured him as they strode around the outer perimeter of the Troskora Arena, through the tunnels that ran beneath the structure. The final showdown would be right above their heads, and while Prince Avalask still wasn't allowed to watch, Izfazara wanted him there to amplify the announcers on the stage.

So in a nearly torturous fate, he was asked to stand behind the wall of the stage where he could listen, and hear all the action, but not see anything.

"Ninkila is a talented fighter, but too nice. Dreya's going to eat her alive," Savaul told him as they heard thousands of feet filing into the arena above to find their places. "We're going to be lucky if we can even keep her from killing poor Ninkila. Dreya doesn't seem to be very coherent when she's in her fighting rage."

Prince Avalask's chest was tight with anticipation — this sounded like exactly the opposite of what he wanted in a mate. He liked... *intellect*, and understanding, and witty banter. He liked clever humor and reflective pondering. It was almost devastating that the competitions were just going to give him a war machine. He tried to remind himself this was what mattered — that she was strong enough to live through the curse and give him a child. And not just any child, but the strongest they could possibly create...

But it was still disappointing that he might have to marry somebody with whom he shared nothing in common. Somewhere, in a place so deep in his heart it was nearly embarrassing, he'd hoped he could have a mate who lit the world for him in a new way. He'd hoped for the love that a thousand years of songs and stories all promised existed.

"Tell me about Ninkila," he said as they climbed up several winding flights of stairs on their way to the upper stage.

121

"She's the pretty, clever one," Savaul told him. "But she's also the underdog, Avalask. I wouldn't place my money on her."

"Smarts matter in a fight," Prince Avalask told him, already hoping Ninkila could pull off what sounded to be a miracle.

Savaul just laughed in return and said, "Not when your opponent is the size of a bear and can strangle you with one hand behind her back."

Prince Avalask tried to think of other things as he accompanied Savaul and Gataan out to the upper stage to look out across the entire arena, joining Gramsaf and Izfazara as the stadium cheered at their arrival. The whole gargantuan arena was *packed*, holding at least twice the Escalis it had been designed to accommodate.

"Prince Avalask?" Izfazara asked, and Prince Avalask gestured to say they could speak to the masses.

Izfazara was a naturally gifted speaker, and knew how to sound both regal and exciting as he called, "Welcome, Escalis, to the final rounds to select our new Epic's wife. Prince Avalask? Tell us honestly. How much of the competitions have you peeked in to watch?"

The crowd chittered their amusement as Prince Avalask gave a breath of a laugh and answered, "As tempted as I've been, there has been no peeking. Although, Savaul can't seem to keep a secret to save his life and has tipped me off about a few things."

Savaul wore a great grin as the crowds laughed more openly. This was something most of the family was quite good at — making all Escalis feel like they were part of the royal family, like they were included in the jokes and knew each of them on a personal level.

Savaul was as talented as Izfazara when it came to stage presence. He'd make a good king one day, with the exception of his unrelenting hatred of Humanity.

"Are you nervous?" Izfazara asked in a stage whisper.

"*Is he nervous?*" Savaul mocked. "Look at him, Uncle. He's

122

shaking."

Prince Avalask folded his arms as the whole arena snickered. They all had eyesight good enough to see Savaul was telling the truth, and Prince Avalask replied, "Perhaps a bit nervous."

The Escalis all laughed openly at that understatement, and even Gramsaf and Gataan were grinning at his misfortune as Gramsaf said, "Alright, let's get him off the stage and get these competitions going."

The whole arena burst into cheers, and Savaul gestured for Prince Avalask to lead the way, as though planning to escort him backstage.

"No looking," Savaul reminded him, and Prince Avalask gave an irritated snort in response. He settled down to sit with his back against the wall, and he kept the voices on the other side of the barrier amplified as their announcer called out the names of both Dreya and Ninkila. They were making a whole show of it as they allowed each combatant's family out to be seen by the people and wish their daughters the best.

He twisted his hands tightly together as the fight finally commenced.

He would hear the crowd cheer and then groan, and the announcer was making it seem certain Dreya had the situation under control.

"Come on, Ninkila," he whispered as the roar of an excited, exuberant stadium rattled the stones beneath his feet.

"And they're in the dirt! It looks like Dreya's got her!" the announcer called, "Ninkila's not going to be able — oooh!" The whole crowd gasped as *something* happened, and Prince Avalask almost couldn't keep himself from looking. "And she's back down!"

Prince Avalask listened out to the cheering instead, and as he focused in on the specific voices, he began to realize nearly every one of them was calling for Dreya to win. It was almost unanimous — the whole arena wanted her to come out on top.

Prince Avalask thought they would know him better than that. He'd thought the Escalis would wish for him to get the beautiful intellect rather than the man-eater.

"And Ninkila's out cold! Dreya wins!" he heard with a sinking feeling. Prince Avalask didn't know why he'd placed his hopes in Ninkila. This was the reason he wasn't supposed to be here, so he wouldn't realize what he'd missed out on.

"Let's get that girl up here!"

The thunderous cheers never stopped, and he heard as a woman's voice joined the others on the stage.

Dreya.

She was throwing joyous thanks out to every Escali as their applause stayed just as raucous as when it started. "You all helped get me here! I've met so many wonderful people, and I will continue to meet more as I take on the journey of a lifetime."

He'd expected a deep, gruff tone, but her voice was pleasantly warm and cheerful. It was a consolation that she at least sounded nice.

The whole crowd was starting to yell some variation of, "Bring him out!" and Savaul appeared suddenly through the doorway.

"Come on," Savaul said, his face alive with excitement. "Come out and meet her!"

"Here?" Prince Avalask demanded. He wasn't supposed to meet her until tomorrow. He wasn't supposed to see her at all before the wedding.

"The crowd demands it," Savaul said, grabbing Prince Avalask's arm to lift him to his feet as the Epic realized his palms were suddenly, distressingly sweaty.

"We're not supposed to do this today —"

"Izfazara gave me the nod to come get you," Savaul insisted.

124

"Now you get to see everything I've been telling you."

Prince Avalask obviously had enough powers at his disposal that he could have stopped Savaul from taking him onto the stage, but if Izfazara had given Prince Avalask the go ahead to come out, then the Escalis were not going to leave this arena until he came out.

It was only his brother's encouragement that got him moving — if not for Savaul's tight grip, he'd still be standing frozen in the hall.

He steeled himself as they neared the arched entry to the arena stage. It wasn't the crowd that bothered him — he usually found thousands of watchers electrifying and drank the energy it gave him to be in front of the masses. No, the terrifying part was that he was about to meet the one he was going to marry, and love, and have a child with. He was about to meet the woman he would inevitably lose.

"Close your eyes," Savaul said, his voice giddy as a spring made his every step bouncy.

"*I will not,*" Prince Avalask retorted indignantly.

"Come on," Savaul shook him roughly. "I'll guide you. Put it off as long as you can, Prince Avalask. She's truly the ugliest of them all."

Prince Avalask was positive Savaul was joking to some degree, but was still mildly terrified of what he was going to find. He squeezed his eyes tightly closed as Savaul pulled him out to the raucous cheers of the Escalis filling the stadium. He'd never heard a crowd so loud or excited.

Prince Avalask couldn't wait another moment, and opened his eyes to see Gramsaf and Izfazara on either side of the woman he'd marry. The three of them had been facing out to the crowd, but turned to look over their shoulders and see him, and his feet stopped moving and ceased to function as he caught his first look.

The first thing he saw was Dreya's smile — warm, full of elation, soaking in the attention from the roaring crowds around them, but also… sweet and inviting as she met his gaze. And she was the size of a regular woman — not any of the massive animals Savaul had compared her to.

Savaul was a lying *snake*.

He froze in awe as he took in the rest of her — her deep brown hair was elaborately braided and tied behind her head, and even with a sheen of sweat across her body and smudges of dirt across her face, nothing could disguise how pretty she was beneath.

She was *stunning* — he was actually, *physically* stunned.

Every Escali in the crowd saw the awe on his face as he froze in a stupor and took in every detail. Her body was toned and fit, she looked entirely comfortable in front of the eyes of thousands, and she laughed softly at the sight of him — a sound that cut straight through him and numbed his mind even further.

"Prince Avalask, are you blushing?" Dreya chided, her voice affectionate and still loud enough for all to hear as the entire arena burst into laughter. "Don't be nervous. Come out here." She waved invitingly for him to come stand beside her, and he was so shocked by her audacity that he stayed frozen and just about choked as he forgot how to breathe.

He'd never looked like a bigger fool in his life.

Savaul shoved a shoulder into his back to get him moving and laughed, "I've never seen you like this."

And Dreya came back to grab his hand and pull him up to the front of the stage with her. The laughter from the audience was well-intentioned, more out of love for the new couple on the stage than any sort of mockery, but Prince Avalask still knew he was humiliating himself in his sudden inability to function.

"We're glad to see you like her," Izfazara said with a light chuckle as Prince Avalask looked to the hand holding his. He couldn't describe why this was happening — why he felt like he'd

126

been electrocuted by a full bolt of lightning — in a good way, if that made any sense...

"Did you have any words you wanted to share, Prince Avalask?" Gramsaf taunted, taking a great amount of joy from seeing the Epic tongue tied.

What was *wrong* with him?

He just shook his head to say he had nothing to add, and the Escalis all across the Troskora Arena cheered and hollered for them, mixed in with the unending laughter at his shock and loss of words.

"It's very good to meet you as well," Dreya said through a grin, squeezing his hand as she met his eyes again and he looked at the stray hairs that had been pulled from her braids. They'd curled around her face where they'd gotten sweaty and dried, framing her face in ringlets.

She was making sweat beautiful. Of course he couldn't comprehend it!

"We can get off the stage now, if you need a moment," she suggested.

He nodded, and she turned back out to the arena to wave her free hand energetically and throw kisses to them all again. "Thank you, Escalis!" she called as everybody stood and cheered even louder. "Victory has chosen well, and I plan for you to see *much* more of me in the years to come!"

Prince Avalask watched her in a daze before she finally turned to him and said, "Shall we?" She pulled him with her and nearly skipped to the back of the stage as they departed and left the applause behind. "I'm sure this must be a bit of a shock," she said with another musical laugh as she let go of his hand and looked him over. "I know almost everything about you, but you just got your very first impression in front of fifty thousand of our closest friends." He nodded and struggled to find something adequate to respond with. "So? Hopefully your first impression was good?" she

127

asked, waving a sweeping gesture over herself. She wasn't the least bit apologetic about the dirt, sweat, or torn clothes. If anything, they made her smile even brighter.

"You're perfect," he whispered, swallowing for the first time in minutes.

Dreya's grin couldn't be quelled, and she took a step closer to ask, "Do I make you nervous, Prince Avalask?" He didn't know why he took an uncertain step back from her. "Or is it the wedding tomorrow in Dekaron that's got you so skittish? I've heard it's going to be quite the memorable affair."

"All of it, really," Prince Avalask admitted as she laughed lightly again. That sound. He couldn't ever hear enough of it. "Dreya... You do know what you've signed up for, right?"

She waved an unconcerned hand and said, "Of course. You had an entire arena of women who knew what we were signing up for. If this really is to be my end, then I'll meet it gracefully. I'll consider it a great honor."

"You... are the one who honors me," he said, unable to come up with words that sounded remotely intelligent. His witty, humorous responses had all fled.

Savaul was still bouncy with enthusiasm as he caught up to them, and Gataan was still grinning at the fool Prince Avalask had made of himself as he trailed his twin closely.

"I told you she was the ugliest of them all!" Savaul exclaimed. Prince Avalask let go of Dreya to shove his brother back.

"You *snake*," he said, still feeling too elated to possibly be angry. Savaul hunched over in his laughter and Prince Avalask took another look at Dreya as his brain tried to process this reality. He was getting to marry somebody who made his insides squirm with excitement from the very first glance.

"Take us to Dekaron, and I'll help her find her room for the night to get settled in," Savaul said. "You'll need to come back to get the rest of the family and her family too. We wouldn't want them traveling all night to get back to Dekaron for the wedding."

Prince Avalask broke into a scowl and said, "I can transport everyone and still help Dreya find her room—"

"You've already seen her more than you were supposed to," Savaul said, stepping between them with a smirk. "And I need to warn her of all your peculiarities before it's too late."

"Savaul—"

"It's alright," Dreya assured the Epic. "I am quite interested to hear the stories I'm sure your brother has stored up to share with me."

"I'm going to start with one of my favorites too," Savaul assured her. "It's about the time Prince Avalask tried to summon a stream of water to help a nearby village, when instead of summoning the nearest stream, he ended up drawing an entire sewage trough—"

"Savaul!" Prince Avalask cut him off, using magic to silence him.

Dreya gave him a disarming grin and said, "I am most excited to hear the end of that story someday, but for now I *would* like to get to Dekaron to start preparations. I'd prefer to not get married covered in sweat and grime, and it's going to take me ages to wash it all off."

Prince Avalask swallowed and tried to think of *anything* other than imagining what that process might look like.

"Let's be off then."

It was the middle of the night, and Prince Avalask paced up and down the long, extravagant Epic's hall as jitters filled him. He both loved and hated the novelty of these feelings. Not only was he the prince, and the Epic, he was also too clever for his own good and always had a laugh and a taunt at the ready. This woman, Dreya, had stricken him speechless with a smile and an easy laugh of her own.

She was beautiful, intelligent, utterly fearless in front of the masses, and strong enough to beat every other woman in the world for the championship title.

He knew without doubt that she was the truest gem he'd ever met, and he was going to get her killed.

Prince Avalask was certain everybody had some sort of nervousness the night before their wedding, but this was different. He couldn't be the reason she died. There had to be somebody else who would do the job.

Prince Avalask leapt out of his hall and landed outside the room they'd given her for the night. He raised his knuckles to knock, then lowered them again. He released a deep, nervous breath, and finally rapped lightly against the wood.

Dreya took a long moment before she pushed the door open and raised her eyebrows in uncertainty. "Is… everything alright?"

"No," he replied, short of breath. He hadn't realized out on the stage, but she smelled amazing too. He didn't know how fate had given him someone so perfect. "Dreya… I don't want you to die for me. I've been thinking it over, and…"

"Prince Avalask," she reached to gently take his hand. "Come in. I have a story to share with you."

She pulled him into her room, where the smell of her was so powerful it made his head fuzzy.

"Come sit," she said as she pushed the door closed and then pulled him to sit beside her on the rumpled bedsheets. Dreya held both of his hands and released a sweet laugh before she said, "I can see you trying to hold your breath. I'm going to assume you're not here to call this off because you think I'm ugly."

"No," he agreed with a stifled chuckle. "It's more the exact opposite."

He couldn't breathe without feeling intoxicated.

"You smell good to me too," she said, giving a light squeeze to his hands. "This may sound strange, but I'd actually like to tell you a story about how many times throughout my life I've been asked why I wasn't married. I don't know if it's in the hundreds or the thousands — apparently I'm quite marketable, and nobody could fathom the thought of me being a single woman in the world. But my answer was always the same. I was waiting for you."

He smiled in return and said, "We've hardly had a chance to meet—"

"I don't mean I was waiting for the right person. Or waiting for someone like you, Prince Avalask. I mean that I was waiting for *you*. I've had a crush burning in my heart since I was a little girl, when you saved our neighbor out of a rockslide. She told me of how you not only saved her, and stayed to heal her, but you took her pain away. You didn't just numb it — you gave her your own comfort as you took her pain upon yourself. And Prince Avalask, I was *so jealous* that I was not the one caught in that rock slide." He laughed at the humor of it now as she added, "I cannot begin to tell you the extent of my jealousy that *she* had the chance to touch you and know you. I'd only caught a tiny glimpse of you leaving, but my five-year-old self had made up her mind, and I told *everybody* that I was in love with you and going to marry you one day."

He raised his eyebrows in awe of the fact this could really be where it all began for her.

"Everybody laughed at me, of course," she said with an easy smile, remembering fondly back to the times. "But my three older brothers indulged me and helped me learn to fight, so I could one day enter the competitions. Nobody thought I was serious until I reached marrying age and refused to marry. I kept working and saving up for more and more fighting lessons. I traveled our whole continent to seek out the best teachers, and learn from every one of them. I've worked in every city, slept in more barns than I dare to

131

remember, and you know what I learned?" He watched her intently as she said, "I learned that the path to becoming exceptional is riddled with people you never knew you needed. Every single person along the way had a unique wisdom to share if I stayed long enough to learn it, and in the course of my travels, I learned from thousands."

"That's why the crowds were so overwhelmingly cheering in your favor," he said softly, watching as her smile brightened her eyes. "You had friends in every city, every village coming out to support you."

"That would be correct," she said, at least trying to look a bit humble when she was clearly very proud of how many people had shown up. "I knew you wouldn't be bothered by the fact I wasn't from a family of wealth or status. I thought you would see value in a wife who'd worked harder than anyone else for her dream, and who knew the joys and struggles of Escalis everywhere."

"Every time you speak, you sound like you already know me," he said softly.

"It's because I do," she replied shamelessly. "I spoke to everyone I could find who'd ever met you, and there has never lived an Escali more loved than you, Prince Avalask. I never found one single person who spoke ill of you, and every time your family came anywhere near my travels, I would come to watch. You never saw me, but every time I would catch a glimpse of you, I would fall in love again and know my dream was still worth pursuing. Can you guess what it was that made me love you?"

Without missing a beat, he confidently replied, "My flowing locks of beautiful black hair?"

Dreya grinned in return and replied, "Well, that too, of course. But I always fell in love with how bright your eyes were."

That wasn't quite what he expected. "It's a family trait, you know," he assured her. "Everyone in the royal family has the same green eyes."

That was *almost* accurate. Archie's eyes had gone crystal blue — the first time the royal green had ever been overpowered by a trait from outside the family.

"I don't mean the color, although they are quite lovely," she said with a hint of teasing. "I meant they were bright with life. I always saw you looking for the humor to add, to ease tense situations around you. I could see you looking for good, when it's so often easier to grouse and complain. My vision of one day marrying you never faltered, until the day the competitions to marry you were actually announced, along with the very real fate the curse would bring to the winner."

Prince Avalask's shoulders sank as she said, "My whole family came back together to discuss whether I should participate — which was quite the feat in itself, since all my brothers had taken to lives of travel as well. But we honestly didn't deliberate for long before we all came to the same conclusion."

"Which was what?"

"That you alone were not worth dying for." Prince Avalask watched her in true surprise as she said, "However, the people I've met and grown to love across our whole continent, *they* are worth the sacrifice — a hundred times over if I could make it."

Prince Avalask had never known that love could be this instant, or this easy, but there was nothing to it. The more she spoke, the more he was absolutely positive he was in love with her.

"I'm not dying for *you*," she assured him. "What we're doing is far more meaningful. I get to be the mother of the next Epic, and teach him all I know and love of our people. I'm going to give you a son who can fight, Prince Avalask. He'll protect the innocent and save the desperate. The Escalis *need* him."

"Normally I'd say I'd be perfectly happy with a daughter, but... given the circumstances..."

"It's going to be a boy. I promise," Dreya said with a confidence that helped put him at ease. "And then I plan to give you another one. A future king. We'll create a set of rulers who can conquer hearts and enemies with ease."

She met his eyes, however Prince Avalask heard the same hesitation in her head as he had in his own. There were just no guarantees. This sounded like his dream life, and his dream mate, but the odds of her surviving the curse long enough to have two children?

He knew better than to hope.

She turned her eyes to the ground and said, "Everybody makes it sound like I'm the hero for choosing to marry you, but you're the one who will have to carry on in the anguish. All I have to do is... *cease to be,* whereas you have to suffer the loss of a mate. I'm more concerned for you than I am for myself."

He opened his mouth to speak, but found nothing to say in response.

"And that," she squeezed his hand in reassurance, "is why I don't want you to feel guilty. I want us to live the time we have to the fullest, and give the Escalis the very best we can give them. Knowing how the story ends won't make it any less exciting."

Prince Avalask had no idea whether he should curse fate or praise it for bringing him Dreya. How had he never sensed her watching him from the crowds? How had he gone his whole life without finding her?

"Does that make you feel better?" she asked, and he nodded as she set a gentle hand on the side of his face. Who would have guessed the strongest woman in the world would also be tender and kind? "Good. You know, I have to say, I was glad to hear that your first reaction to me was to call me *perfect,*" she said with her warm grin.

"Dreya," he said, not caring who she ever repeated this to, "I

134

could not have dreamed you up better than you are."

"Oh, I do so enjoy a poet," she said as she leaned in to place a sweet kiss on his cheek. He could feel his whole face flush red, with no regard for the fact he was the honorable Prince Avalask with a reputation to uphold. "And I'll have lots more of those for you after we're married tomorrow."

Prince Avalask stood and tried to breathe, feeling like his whole body might actually be on fire. "I..." he choked. "I'll..."

"I'll see you tomorrow," she said with humored affection, sparing him the task of trying to find words.

He nodded, and then leapt away before he could make a further fool of himself.

There was no chance in the world he was going to sleep tonight. He was going to lay awake savoring that kiss until morning came and he got to marry her and to spend the rest of her life making a fool of himself for her. He'd never been more excited and terrified by anything.

Prince Avalask

Chapter Fourteen

The wedding was beautiful and extravagant, and bonding was… *easily* the best two weeks of Prince Avalask's entire life. The bonding process was known to take between eight and fourteen days, but all of his previously married family members warned him to expect a full fourteen.

So for two full weeks, he enjoyed the glorious gift of Escali hormones and pheromones that glued two people together eternally. It was perfect bliss. It was two weeks of passion more intimate than he'd ever imagined, and it was the only time in his life he'd ever been able to live in ignorance of everything happening outside himself.

For two weeks, the Escalis defended themselves, and he got to exist with nothing in the world to think about except Dreya.

Fourteen days passed in what felt like hours, and Prince Avalask had just finally gotten his mind into a clear enough state that he could drag himself into the halls and meet with Gramsaf and Izfazara. Barely.

It was time to hear about the havoc and destruction Avery and the Human mages had caused in his absence.

"Treldinsae took a terrible beating," Gramsaf was telling him, but Prince Avalask could hardly focus. He felt like his entire chest had been ripped open and half of him was… *missing*.

136

Izfazara added, "They've set fire to half our crops down in Raso —"

"*Avalask,*" Gramsaf scolded, snapping him out of his distracted focus as he checked in to make sure Dreya was alright. She was fine, but he couldn't shake the feeling of anxiety wracking his chest. "Are you listening at all?"

Izfazara chuckled and said, "He just finished bonding, Gramsaf. You remember what that was like." Izfazara shook his head and released a sigh. "Go find her, Avalask. You're clearly in a great deal of pain being here. You can have another day."

Prince Avalask didn't even attempt to claim he was alright — he leapt away immediately and landed behind Dreya, who whipped around and pulled him into a tight hug without hesitation.

Prince Avalask tried not to crush her, but holding her as tightly as she could handle was the only thing that started to make him feel whole, like he wasn't melting down in a panic attack.

Dreya released a deep sigh of relief and said, "I thought all the stories of *post-bonding pains* were coward's tales, but I really just felt like I was dying with you gone. I couldn't even survive an afternoon."

Prince Avalask's racing heart finally slowed as he pressed his nose to her hair and the smell of her calmed him. "What did Izfazara and Gramsaf say happened while we were indisposed?" she asked.

"I only caught about a tenth of it," he replied with an exhale of a laugh. "Avery wrecked some stuff, lit some fires —"

"Prince Avalask," she scolded. "You're supposed to care about these things."

"I *do,*" he insisted, "but I couldn't concentrate on anything they said. Izfazara eventually just told me I could come back here, and I didn't argue. I need another day with you. I shouldn't have ventured out."

"That will put us at the full fourteen," she said, tightening her arms around him. "I'm not complaining, but we *will* have to figure out how to live as two individuals again soon."

"Tomorrow," he said, picking her up again to carry her back to bed. "We'll figure it out tomorrow."

Prince Avalask woke up in the morning and untangled himself from Dreya as he lay back to stare at the ceiling in a moment of thought.

He was pretty sure he could make it through most of the day without her, but there was a much bigger problem weighing on his chest now.

If she died, he was going to drop dead too. His heart beat in time with hers. Being apart for even a couple hours caused real, physical pain. There would be no surviving it if he lost her.

He finally got up and pulled on black clothes, and his long cloak of black fur around his shoulders. He left and made it through his entire meeting with Gramsaf, Izfazara, Savaul, and Gataan as his brothers laughed at his still-wandering focus.

He leapt out to Raso with Izfazara to reassure the Escalis that they'd be taken care of since their crops for the year were in ruins. They leapt to Treldinsae where Prince Avalask helped rebuild the walls — this was far from the first time he'd helped piece Treldinsae back together. And he visited the injured among them as Dreya's thoughts reached him as though she were standing next to him.

What are you doing? she asked straight into his mind.

Helping those who were injured in the Treldinsae attacks, he replied as he traded feeling with a young woman on the cot beside him and grimaced at the agony he now felt in her place.

Come get me. I want to be there.

It's not a pretty scene out here…

138

Prince Avalask, do I strike you as a woman who married you to live pretty?

"I'll be right back," he said to the Escali he'd been helping, and she nodded as she braced herself for the return of the pain. Prince Avalask leapt and grabbed Dreya to bring her to Treldinsae.

He returned to the bedside of the young woman as Dreya looked all around the room full of injured and called, "Somebody give me a job to do."

The two closest healers looked to each other in shock before they both looked back to Dreya. "That's alright, your highness," the first woman said. "We don't have anything fitting—"

"I know how to change a bedpan," Dreya said with a scowl. "I can carry people in. Give me something to do. Just because I'm married to the man who does everything, doesn't mean I don't *do* things anymore."

They finally settled on allowing her to distribute water to those who needed it.

This is ridiculous, she thought to Prince Avalask as she helped people drink. *They gave me the easiest, cleanest job in the whole place. I don't mind getting my hands dirty.*

Get used to it, he thought back to her. *People will always try to serve and please you, wherever you go.*

But I came to help—

Even when you've come to help, he thought back as she rolled her eyes.

"I don't need any water," the next man told her.

Yes he does, Prince Avalask thought, trying not to smirk as Dreya simply replied, "Yes you do. You're not inconveniencing me by accepting the water I'm bringing around."

"I'm simply not thirsty—"

"Prince Avalask says you are, so stop fighting me and take a drink," Dreya snapped, and the man immediately drank from the ladle she held.

Prince Avalask watched in amusement as Dreya finished passing out water, then marched outside to help carry people in. They stayed in Treldinsae most of the night, before Prince Avalask had to leave to prevent Sir Avery from tearing into a traveling caravan.

"Haven't seen you in a while," Sir Avery called before Prince Avalask threw him back into the trees and leapt after him. It was almost customary for them to exchange a short quip now, every time they met in battle.

Their battle ended unspectacularly, and Prince Avalask looked back in on Dreya before he leapt to Treldinsae, only to see she'd taken a strong role in running the operation. Multiple people knew her and were delighted to have her assistance, and she was moving among the gathered Escalis with purpose, giving orders to everyone who wanted to help but didn't know how.

"We have too many Escalis and not enough beds. Go to your homes and bring all the blankets and makings for somewhere to lay our wounded. You there, come help carry people in, and you head out to the well for fresh water."

She found jobs for every Escali in the vicinity, and nobody even hesitated. They clearly respected and adored Dreya, either because she'd met them in her travels or they knew her from the competitions. She may as well have been born into the royal family for how eager everyone was to please her and gain her praise. It sparked life and hope into the whole area, just having her present.

The thought of losing her crossed his mind again, and how greatly it would affect not only Prince Avalask, but every Escali everywhere. Losing Dreya would crush *all* their spirits.

There was only one thing to do. He knew the cost to expect, but he'd do anything necessary to keep her alive.

Prince Avalask leapt, but instead of reappearing in Dekaron, he reappeared outside the ring of firelight flickering against the grey clothes and white cloaks of five powerful Human men.

Maverick, Prince Avalask thought to him, and Maverick turned his eyes away from the fire to where Prince Avalask stood further back in the trees. The years had turned Maverick into an even colder, somehow more frightening version of the man he'd been when Prince Avalask last spoke to him. Ten years had passed since the night Archie was born. Navvad had retired from the Zhauri and Maverick was the leader of the group now.

May we speak? Prince Avalask asked.

"You may come to the fire," Maverick replied aloud.

The other four Zhauri looked attentively to where Maverick's eyes had settled, and Prince Avalask hesitated, just beyond their line of sight.

Maverick still had Hakkrui, whose powers in stopping motion had gotten even stronger with Maverick in charge of their trainings. But Maverick had brought two new members onto the team as well — Zeen and Iquis — and Prince Avalask had seen the things they could do. Iquis could mentally cripple anyone. Zeen was the Zhauri's new interrogator, who thought torture was some sort of art form, and considered himself a master of the craft.

The Zhauri under Maverick's leadership were even stronger and crueler than they'd been before, and a part of him wanted to jump away before it was too late.

But he couldn't. This was the only chance in the world he had to save Dreya.

Prince Avalask stepped into their sight as the fire crackled and everybody but Maverick tensed at the sight of him.

Maverick looked up with disinterest, but Prince Avalask could feel a cool rage building beneath his calm. "I wondered when we'd

141

be seeing you," Maverick said, pulling one of the hidden blades from his sleeve to sharpen it without concern. "The curse is snapping and flickering like it finally has purpose again. On an unrelated note, how is your new wife's health? She faring well?"

Prince Avalask released a pent up breath, and simply said, "I'll do anything. Name your price, and I'll pay it."

Maverick smiled coolly to himself — an expression that sank Prince Avalask's hopes. "I've been thinking on it, Avalask," Maverick said without emotion, "and I'm not sure there's anything you can do at this point to earn my forgiveness. I've missed out on *ten* years of my son's, or possibly daughter's, life already. I don't mind waiting a few more before I find him myself." Maverick tossed a small twig into the fire and added as an afterthought, "I hope you don't mind I'm going to assume I had a son, since I think the curse would have already killed her if she were a girl."

"I'll play along with you assuming it's a boy," Prince Avalask said, careful to keep his mind closely guarded from being read. He'd gotten better at protecting his thoughts over the past ten years. "But you won't find him without me. I guarantee it."

"I guarantee you're wrong."

"I'll bring him to you," Prince Avalask said. He'd known all along this was what it would take.

"Full of warnings about how terrible, manipulative, and tyrannical I am, I'm sure," Maverick added for him. He raised his eyebrows and asked, "What have you told him of me?"

"Very little," Prince Avalask replied.

"I see." Maverick turned his attention back to his knife sharpening, as though this conversation held no interest to him whatsoever. "So you'll bring me my own child, allow me an hour to see him, and then be off again? I don't think so."

"I'll leave him with you. I'll never return, and never contact him again. I'll say anything you want me to. I'll say I kidnapped him at

142

birth—"

"That is exactly what you did," Maverick replied darkly. "You may go now. I'll consider your proposal. Come back in a few days' time, on your knees, and I'll see if I can find it in myself to accept."

"Maverick, I'm trying to give you exactly what you want—"

"Your invitation to sit by our fire is expiring," Maverick said, holding his blade up to check the edge. "If you're still here in another minute, I'm going to let Zeen and Iquis show you just how much pain we've discovered the Escali body can handle."

Prince Avalask snarled in return before he turned to leap away.

"And don't think that's a suggestion, Avalask," Maverick added, meeting his gaze for one last chilling moment. "Return here on your knees or not at all."

He landed back in the Obsidian Tower as Dreya approached him cautiously, frowning in concern as she saw the fury on his face. "Where did you go?" she asked.

Just being close to her calmed him as he released a pent-up breath of anger. He suddenly understood how Gramsaf could be vicious toward the whole world, but always softened when their mother was around. The very sight and smell of Dreya drained his anger.

"I went to Maverick," he admitted.

Dreya's face lit with alarm as she asked, "Why? You weren't trying to get the curse, were you?"

"I... tried to barter with him for it. I offered to bring him Archie. I thought that was what he wanted."

Dreya was trying to guess where that had gotten him, and ventured, "Archie wasn't enough?"

"He said he'd think about it," Prince Avalask replied. "He knows Archie's only ten. I think he's planning to wait a few years

143

and then go after him, when he has a competent young man to manipulate and mold."

"I don't want you trading Archie to him for my sake," Dreya said. "If he's as wicked as you say..."

"It may not even be an option," Prince Avalask said through a scowl. "He told me that if I came back on my knees, he might consider taking Archie in exchange for the curse—"

"Maverick can go rot in a fire-filled dunghole," Dreya spat in return as Prince Avalask widened his eyes in surprise. "And if he ever comes near you, I'll be the one to put him there. I do not want you going back to him. I will not have you groveling to that snake, or offering to give him Glidria's son in exchange for my wellbeing."

"I still feel like I'm just getting to know you," Prince Avalask said through a hint of a laugh. "I thought you were kind and sweet—"

"Sweet girls don't make it far in this world without learning to be spicy," she retorted. "How do you think I won the tournament to marry you, Prince Avalask? You think I outcharmed the competition?"

"That was my initial guess—"

"You and I haven't fought yet," she suddenly declared. "Get us a pair of sparring staffs. I'll show you what kind and sweet can do."

He raised his hands defensively and asked, "Do I get to use magic?"

"*No.*"

"Then no thank you," he replied as her scowl made him want to laugh. He wrapped his arms around her instead and said, "I'm sure you'd be the winner. There's no need to embarrass me by proving it."

"You remember that," she said as she hugged him tightly back. "It was still hard being apart today," she admitted as she pressed her face into him.

"I know. It was for me too."

It didn't matter how many hours they spent together, it could never be enough.

CHAPTER FIFTEEN

rince Avalask just had to open his ears to the world to find where he was needed, and he reached for Dreya's hand as he leapt and reappeared beside a clay house in the western deserts, surrounded by golden sand.

He knocked lightly and felt confusion inside as a young Escali girl came to pull the door open. She screamed as she saw Prince Avalask and Dreya in the doorway, and took a shocked step back before she quickly knelt. "It's P-Prince Avalask, and Princess Drey-Dreya," she stuttered as a man and woman emerged quickly from the back room.

"*Oh holy life,*" the mother exclaimed as they both quickly knelt as well. "Are you here to help?"

A naked little toddler of a boy sprinted happily out of the side room, chased by an older brother who saw their guests at the door and just about tripped and fell over in horror.

"Tirran! Tirran, get down!" he hissed as he scrambled after the naked runner to pull him into a kneel as well.

"It's alright," Prince Avalask said holding a hand out to tell them they didn't have to kneel, finding the chaos both funny and endearing as Dreya chuckled behind him. "We both feel very respected. Everybody can stand. You have another daughter who's sick?"

146

"Yes, back here," the mother of the four stood quickly and gestured him back. "Her name is Areese, and we've been trying to give her water but she's stopped drinking it—"

"We think it's feather fever," the father added.

"I'm pretty sure you're right," Prince Avalask agreed as he accompanied them to the back room. The whole family of six had darkened skin, a common feature among Escalis who lived beneath the harsh sun of the western desert, but the girl before him had a deep red flush to her cheeks. She was in worse shape than he'd hoped to find.

Prince Avalask reached to summon a chair, and pulled it up to sit beside her. The parents and older sister came in to watch, and the oldest brother finally joined them after wrestling his little brother into a pair of pants.

Prince Avalask didn't mind that the tiny room was cramped and full of people, he just needed his full concentration to see what was wrong with the young girl before him.

It *was* feather fever, a sickness carried by birds that affected its victim's blood. If he'd heard their distress earlier, he would have absolutely been able to stop its spread, but now… He wasn't sure if he could.

How bad? Dreya asked straight into his mind.

I don't know if I can save her or not, he admitted. *Are you alright if we stay most of the night?*

Dreya just gave him a short head tilt, as though she couldn't believe that was a real question. *Of course.*

The older sister kept glancing at Dreya, and Dreya met her next glance with a grin. "What's your name, girl?"

"Driikyn," she answered quickly, looking guiltily away.

"Driikyn, you have such lovely dark hair. I hope you don't mind that I simply cannot help myself." Dreya didn't even ask — she just moved behind Driikyn and reached to her side to withdraw a comb

147

Prince Avalask hadn't even realized she was carrying. Driikyn seemed utterly shocked as Dreya combed through a section of her hair, and began to braid it elaborately back in the fashion she'd worn during the tournament.

"Is Areese going to die?" Driikyn asked, looking back to Dreya in despair. "Is that why you're being so nice?"

"Believe it or not, I actually just love giving young ladies combat-braids. You won't believe how strong it makes you feel, having your hair done up like a warrior's." Driikyn winced as Dreya tugged out a stubborn piece of hair and combed through it. "Although, I will admit it is my job to keep everybody distracted so Prince Avalask can focus most clearly on his work." He caught her eyes and gave her a hint of a grateful smile. "So talk to me, Driikyn. Tell me of something I could do as a new member of the royal family that would be to the benefit of our great people."

The girl frowned for a long moment of thought, then her eyes brightened with an idea. "You could let Narrik join the royal guard." Driikyn shot her older brother a sideways smirk as his jaw fell open. "He's dreamed of it his whole life. Makes me train with him all the time."

"Is that so?" Dreya asked with a grin. "And are you any good, Narrik?"

"I... think I am," he replied, still seeming a bit starstruck to be in the room with *both* Prince Avalask and Dreya.

"Then let's go outside. You can show me," Dreya said.

"But we... your majesty..." he stuttered. "We don't have any weapons worthy of your hands." Narrik fumbled to find his words. "We just... use a couple well-balanced sticks we found when we traveled to the forest."

"I don't need it to be solid silver, Narrik. I learned with a few brothers and a well-balanced stick as well. I'd like to see what you can do. Also, my job here is still to be the distraction, so indulge

148

me." Dreya finished the braid in her fingers and tugged playfully on it. "You come too," she told Driikyn. "I'm quite certain our royal guard would benefit if we added a few women to it."

"ME TOO!" the youngest boy added at the top of his lungs.

"Well, of course," Dreya said, rattling Driikyn's shoulders as she stepped toward the littlest guy. "Tirran, is it? We would be honored for you to join us." She gave Prince Avalask an innocent smile as she reached to hold Tirran's hand and said, "The three of us will be outside."

Thank you, he thought to her.

I'll keep them busy long enough for you to talk to the parents.

Driikyn and Narrik took another look at their sick sister, Areese, before they left with Dreya. "Prince Avalask will let us know if anything changes," she told them as little Tirran led the way, showing her exactly how to get to the outside.

Prince Avalask sighed as he set one hand on the little girl's face, and her cheek burned angrily beneath his touch.

"You can tell us now," her father said, watching with worry as Areese exhaled a low, painful moan. "Is she going to be alright?"

"We'll know by morning," Prince Avalask replied. Areese shifted to hug his arm like he was her own stuffed doll she was cuddling up to for safety. She was adorable. He knew he couldn't let her family lose her.

"We've heard stories of your kindness," her mother said softly, leaning in to brush Areese's hair out of her face. "But... To stay all night, at the bedside of a girl you've never met, who may not even make it..."

"We are very fortunate to have you," her father said softly, resting his chin on closed fists. "I mean all Escalis. We are all very fortunate."

"Believe me, this is the part of being an Epic I relish most," Prince Avalask replied as he set his second hand on Areese's

149

feverish neck. "I've always found it a shame to see Epics waste their lives in combat. This is more rewarding."

Areese opened her eyes for a moment and squinted in uncertainty.

"Prince... Avalask?" she asked. A sudden horror overcame her as she realized she hadn't knelt for him.

"No, stop, it's alright," he said with amusement as she tried to roll off the bed and he held her in place. "You don't have to do anything. I'm here to help *you*."

Areese looked to her parents' worried faces and then back up to Prince Avalask. "You're... going to make me feel better?"

"That's right."

"Can I go back to sleep?" she asked softly. He nodded and was about to say *yes* as she added, "Right after I give you something."

She reached to grab his face and pull him closer, and she give him a soft kiss on the cheek before she settled back down and closed her eyes again and muttered, "Thank you."

Prince Avalask just about had to hold a tear back as he gritted his teeth. This didn't change anything. He still didn't know if he could save her. But he wanted to, *so badly*.

Prince Avalask turned his attention outside, just in time to see Dreya duck beneath Narrik's high swing, and she kicked his feet right out from beneath him. Dreya was back up in a flash as Narrik recovered from landing flat on his back, and Dreya whipped around as Driikyn struck at her from behind.

Prince Avalask suddenly couldn't believe he'd never seen her fight — she made it look like dancing as she spun and whirled her staff-sized stick like a baton. She maneuvered herself behind Driikyn and planted a foot in the girl's back, shoving her to the ground next to Narrik.

Then she turned her attention to Tirran, who was only as tall as her thighs.

"You want a turn?" she asked him.

Tirran nodded happily as he picked up a stick far too large to be of any use. "You let me win?" he asked with an excited grin.

"Oh no, I will not be letting you win," Dreya replied with an inviting gesture. "I will let you strike first though."

Holy life, Dreya, go easy on him! Prince Avalask thought out to her.

I will not, Dreya thought back, readying herself for the little guy to strike. *If he thinks he can beat the world-renowned Dreya at the ripe age of two, what is there left for him to work toward?*

Narrik and Driikyn's faces both filled with fear as Tirran ran forward and swung at Dreya.

Dreya reached and grabbed the stick mid-swing and jerked it back from his grasp. And then she lunged and picked him up, holding him upside down as she tickled him. Tirran laughed out of control and tried to break free as she chided, "You're going to have to learn to hit a bit harder, little Tirran. It would be *terribly* embarrassing if your enemies could pick you up and tickle you."

Dreya turned him right-side up again and gave him a second to catch his breath as she moved him to rest on her hip. "Are the two of you going to come rescue your brother or what?" she demanded as they both scrambled back to their feet and grabbed the sticks they'd each dropped.

"Hold on tight," Dreya whispered to Tirran as he giggled and clung tightly to her. "I'll show you what a fight looks like from a winner's perspective."

"We don't want to hit him," Driikyn exclaimed as she and Narrik prowled around to either side of Dreya.

"Don't worry," Dreya said with an easy laugh of pure confidence. She spun her stick like a performer again and said, "You won't."

Prince Avalask laughed to himself as he watched Narrik and Driikyn fail to come anywhere close.

Narrik struck first and Dreya countered with such a sharp counterstrike, she knocked his weapon straight from his hands. In the same motion, she leapt and kicked at Driikyn's strike, parrying it with a high kick as Narrik retrieved his weapon and tried to hit her from behind.

Tirran held on tightly as she performed every move like she was on a stage in a choreographed battle, and he giggled each time she would knock a weapon from his brother and sister's hand. He laughed long and hard when she kicked Narrik to the ground for a second time.

Prince Avalask watched Dreya with more love than he knew how to handle, unable to resist admiring every strike and the tenderness with which she held Tirran as she protected him from the blows of the other two. If he weren't already holding something precious in his hands, he would have pranced outside to join the battle, to show Narrik and Driikyn that *somebody* could still stand up to her prowess.

She was going to be the best mother in the world. He almost didn't want to wait.

Maybe it was because the thought was already on his mind, but he glanced and realized with a sudden pang of fear...

They didn't have too long to wait after all.

Dreya was already pregnant.

Prince Avalask and Dreya stayed at the clay desert home all night until the little girl's fever finally broke and her face began to return to its normal, desert-tinted brown. Dreya had done quite an impressive job of wearing out Driikyn, Narrik, and Tirran. All three of them were asleep on the floor of Areese's room by the time Prince Avalask stood and rubbed at his tired eyes.

He and Dreya bid their parents farewell, and Dreya asked in his head if they could stop in the courtyard behind the Obsidian Tower before heading to bed. They landed in Dekaron a minute later, and Prince Avalask frowned as she took off toward the shed where they housed a whole assortment of practice weapons.

"Aren't you ready for bed?" Prince Avalask asked, wondering if she could seriously be hoping to spar with him now too.

"Very ready. But first," Dreya opened the doors and pulled out a dulled, double-bladed practice staff. She found a second one to match it, and then handed them to him. "Reappear these outside their house. They'll know who sent them."

Prince Avalask smiled to himself then vanished the staves from her grip, sending them to the clay house in the desert. "You thought they had some potential then?" He reached for her hand and leapt them up to their shared room of black glass walls in the Obsidian Tower.

"They were both pretty rough, but I see potential in everyone. Sometimes you've just got to give them combat braids, or gift them a real practice staff for them to realize they've got something worth honing."

"Good life, I love you," he said, unable to keep it in any longer. "Can I tell you something?"

Dreya frowned, and all Prince Avalask did was flick his eyes down to her stomach, then back up again with an excited grin, and her eyes widened in immediate understanding.

"Really?" she exclaimed. She jumped in place and put her hands over her mouth as she laughed aloud. "Prince Avalask, this is —"

She stopped as an eerie squeaking sound echoed around them, like ice being splintered apart. And Prince Avalask realized in a moment of panic that massive cracks were spreading through the glass floor beneath them.

"Dreya!" He lunged to grab her as the entire outside wall and half the floor gave way and the fractured glass broke away from the

153

rest of the tower.

He held her up in mid-air with a shield around them both, just in case the ceiling decided to fracture apart next. The floor they'd been standing on fell and crashed to the ground, far below, sending another score of cracks through the black obsidian.

Dreya looked down at the empty air beneath and breathed, "Has that *ever* happened before?"

"No," he replied in horrified disbelief, "and this tower is hundreds of years old."

He leapt and reappeared with her out on the outskirts of the city, inside a vacant, *sturdy*, one-story farmhouse.

"That was the curse, wasn't it?" Dreya asked as she looked all about the room. "It can influence seemingly random events. I mean… part of the tower was probably on the brink of collapsing anyway, but the curse made the fracture happen while I was in it."

"That's exactly what just happened," Prince Avalask replied, raising his hand to chew absentmindedly at his thumbnail. He paced back and forth until Dreya approached to set her hand on his shoulder. He felt instantly calmer, but it didn't change what was happening. "This is just the beginning," he said, reaching around the room to pull all the old ragged curtains closed with magic.

Dreya exhaled a laugh and said, "What's that going to do?" She moved to pull the curtains back open. "The sunlight isn't going to attack me next."

He waved a hand and closed the curtains again as he said, "It could be a stray arrow, or somebody could see us and attack…"

Dreya pulled the curtains open again with a challenging raise of her eyebrows. "I'm not going to live in a cave, Prince Avalask," she said sternly. "There's nothing here to collapse on me, there are no stray arrows being fired, and if anyone decides to attack me in here, I am more than capable of defending myself." He narrowed his eyes as she lowered her voice to growl, *"Leave them open."*

154

Prince Avalask lay awake as Dreya fell asleep, and he stared at the ceiling in anxious worry.

After an hour of listening to her breathing, he climbed out of bed, pulled his black cloak around his shoulders, and went to find Maverick again.

Prince Avalask would have just grabbed Archie and brought him if he weren't certain Maverick would have demands about what he wanted Prince Avalask to tell him. Poor Archie. Prince Avalask didn't want this life for his sister's son, but... Dreya's life — his own son or daughter's life — now depended on him striking a deal with Maverick.

I came back, he said as Maverick looked up from the map in his hands, where the other Zhauri were huddled around, trying to pinpoint where their current target would have most likely headed.

Maverick just flicked his eyes up to the sky in annoyance, and told the other Zhauri, "We need to take a break for just a minute. Avalask. Approach."

Prince Avalask approached them warily, very aware of Iquis's hungry eyes fixated on him, like he was the man's next meal.

"What did I ask?" Maverick said with a look cold enough to freeze an ocean.

Prince Avalask's whole body just about revolted as he forced himself to do something he'd never done for anyone in his life. He lowered himself onto his knees, and gritted his teeth at the feeling of vulnerability before the Zhauri, who were all still standing.

"I'm here," he said as a deep discomfort sank through him, "and I will get you the thing you want most."

He *hated* this. No Escali ever felt like this when they knelt for the royal family. They knelt as a gesture of respect — not to feel like they were vulnerable and groveling at a superior's feet.

155

"Actually, Avalask, I've had a little time to think it over," Maverick said, rolling the map in his hands into a tidy little scroll, "and I don't actually care for children one bit. I have no need for a ten-year-old tagging along and slowing our brotherhood down."

"A ten-year-old half-Escali is more like your version of fourteen," Prince Avalask argued. "We're not talking about a child anymore."

"I'll wait a few more years until I have a real young man or woman to train," Maverick said without emotion. "You have my condolences for the loss you're about to suffer."

"Maverick, I *can't* lose her," Prince Avalask said as his pride rotted beneath the shame of being on his knees ready to beg. "I can get you anything you could ever—"

"Here's what you're not understanding," Maverick cut him off. "I have everything I could ever want. What matters is that you crossed me. You will regret that decision for the rest of your life, Avalask, and I expect it to *never* happen again."

"We're not enemies, Maverick, not yet," Prince Avalask lowered his voice to a much more threatening tone. "And trust me — you don't want me as your enemy."

Maverick released a loud, malicious laugh in return, and Prince Avalask's entire body filled with rage as Maverick said, "You are sadly mistaken on both counts. We have been enemies since the night Glidria died, and you do not frighten me one bit. Now why don't you go spend some quality time with your dying wife before you lose her. I'm sure it won't take long—"

Prince Avalask leapt to his feet and lunged toward the terrible Human before his more cautious side could warn him against the mistake.

Hakkrui stopped his motion in an instant, and he released a sharp scream as Iquis drilled excruciating mental pain to flare through every nerve in his body.

156

It was so blinding, so numbing, that he couldn't even muster a thought in response, let alone leap away or summon a single power against it.

But he did hear a low laugh from Maverick as he told the others, "This was about what I expected." Prince Avalask felt hands picking him up as Maverick added, "Let's see if we can't make you regret that too, shall we?"

Prince Avalask lost all concept of time and how much of it passed. There was only blinding pain, and an undeterminable number of hours that they had him out, unconscious.

And they'd taken him somewhere.

Prince Avalask awoke with his hands locked into gloves and tied behind his back. He was choking on a rag they'd stuffed in his mouth and he couldn't vanish, or push himself to his feet, or free his hands — none of his powers were working.

He was on the ground and could hear a general commotion around him as he struggled to get free, or get his powers to work. Hands flipped him over, and then there were Escalis above him, just about frantic with worry as they realized who they'd found.

"It's Prince Avalask," the hushed whispers spread quickly as they untied his feet and got the gag out of his mouth. He coughed and sputtered as they quickly moved to untie his hands too, and that's when he saw Savaul, Gataan, and Dreya running out to him, pushing hastily through the gathering crowd.

"Avalask!" Dreya exclaimed, dropping immediately next to him to grab his face in her hands. "Are you alright?"

He nodded quickly as his hands came free and he pulled them around to see the gloves still locked onto each hand. They were the culprits keeping him from using physical magic. All he had were mind powers with these gloves on.

"Avalask, they just walked straight into the city!" Savaul exclaimed as Gataan stood watch behind him, as though ready for the Zhauri to return. "The five of them. Straight through the streets of Dekaron, and there was nothing we could do."

"That was Maverick, wasn't it?" Dreya asked in despair. "You went back to him to try to get the curse?"

"Just give him that shanking Tally son he wants!" Savaul exclaimed.

"I was trying to," Prince Avalask spat back, rubbing his bruised wrists. "But he doesn't want to talk, so now I'm going to kill him."

"At long last," Savaul said, looking over his shoulder to where the Zhauri must have disappeared.

"Avalask," Dreya said, her voice hoarse with scorn. "Look around at what just happened. It is just as likely you'll get yourself killed." The entire avenue was full of onlookers now — Escalis who'd just seen their most esteemed Epic thrown into the street like a sack of turnips. The shame of it was cruel.

"Not this time," he said, moving to get to his feet as Dreya grabbed his hand to help him up. "I acted rashly. I let them get the upper hand. I'll be smarter about it next time."

"Let's get out of the street and get those gloves off you," Savaul said, moving to lead the way as Dreya grabbed Prince Avalask's arm in a tight grip.

With his powers contained beneath the gloves, he realized for the first time how strong she was, and how tightly she could hold a man. Dreya held his hand up and pulled his sleeve back, revealing black ink down his forearm.

In perfect Escalira, Maverick had written,

I don't usually give warnings,
but out of respect to your sister, this is yours.
You won't get a second.

Savaul and Dreya both read the words before he shoved his sleeve back down to his wrist and Savaul simmered with rage.

"I have been waiting half my life for the day we'd plot against that man," Savaul said, meeting Prince Avalask's eyes with determination. "I've had a lot of years to think about creative ways to harm him."

"I'm guessing Gramsaf will have a few good ideas too," Prince Avalask said as he took Dreya's hand and Savaul led the way for them all to retreat back to the Obsidian Tower.

Savaul shot a devious grin back to them and said, "Our father most certainly does. He's been anxiously awaiting this day too. We'll bring that Human down, Avalask, and we'll have that curse broken in no time. Just watch."

Prince Avalask

Chapter Sixteen

Davaul, Gataan, and Gramsaf happily joined Prince Avalask's vendetta. They kept a map laid out across their gigantic dining table where they could examine the Zhauri's movements and keep track of everything they knew about the hunters. Izfazara was highly interested in the outcome as well, although extremely cautious when it came to anything that could possibly endanger Prince Avalask.

They included Iktor, the general who had extensive experience combatting the Human mages — although he'd never faced any as strong as the Zhauri.

They also brought in Rallek, Prince Avalask's old friend and also the new head of the Translation Program. Rallek had recently become the master of all the secret information their translators brought back from their infiltrations into the Human territories. The job had brought out a side of him nobody had ever seen while he was a student. They'd learned quickly that he was an exceptional infiltrator the moment he'd graduated, but it turned out Rallek was also a calculating mastermind with a sharp memory for detail.

"We've got multiple infiltrators out looking for information on the Zhauri — anything we could use against them," Rallek said, looking over the map before them. He kept no notes with him, save the ones he had engrained in his mind. "We've had very little luck locating anyone with reliable information. I only have one lead that I consider promising." He glanced to Prince Avalask and said, "It's not something you're going to like though."

"What did you find?" Savaul asked.

"One of our newer translators, Esrim, says he very strongly believes Maverick's got a second son, hidden up in the north. We think he's just a few years older than Archie, but we haven't been able to locate him."

"Why wouldn't we like that news?" Savaul asked with a frown.

"Because," Prince Avalask answered without looking up from the map, "If we go after his son and threaten his family, then we *are* the Zhauri. What's the point in fighting them if we're exactly the same?"

"The *point* is that your wife's going to die if we don't," Savaul snapped back.

"There are other ways to kill Maverick that don't include targeting children," Prince Avalask retorted. He already regretted that he'd been willing to hand Archie over to his father, and dragging another of Maverick's sons into the mix was no better. "Keep looking, Rallek. The information is good, but we need more."

"Avalask," Gramsaf said with his brows lowered incredulously. "Going after the things they care about might be your only option. They are *impossible* to reach otherwise."

"Not impossible," Prince Avalask said, nodding to Iktor. "The general has some ideas."

"Ideas, yes," Iktor agreed. "There are a few things that I think could work, but it depends on how strong the Zhauri are. I think we could collapse a cliff face onto them, but if we believe Rallek's rumors, then that stop-motion mage could stop an entire mountain worth of rocks. We could try to drown them, but I think the stop-motion might be able to stop the water."

"Their stop-motion is vulnerable to mind attacks," Gramsaf said.

"Yes," Iktor agreed, "but if Prince Avalask attacks mentally and Iquis joins the mental fight, he could kill our Epic with a thought. Mind attacks are too dangerous to consider."

"We'll try everything," Prince Avalask said. "Even Humanity's most dangerous have to have weaknesses. Declaring war on the most powerful Escalis is going to be the end of them."

The Escali royal family put into motion multiple attempts to kill the Zhauri, but the Human mages were incredibly resilient.

Prince Avalask waited until they were traveling through the mountain crevices of the north before he collapsed an entire cliffside onto them — but Iktor had been correct. Hakkrui stopped every falling rock in midair and allowed them to pass unhindered. He was also able to stop the flood of water Prince Avalask tried to unleash on them, and not even a single member of the Zhauri brotherhood got water in his boots.

The Escalis got especially devious and dirty as they poisoned the wildlife the Zhauri would inevitably hunt for their dinners, but Maverick sensed the intent before any of them took a bite. Nobody even suffered a hint of indigestion, and Maverick also felt the intent when Prince Avalask tried to set fire to their lodging in the middle of the night to suffocate them in the smoke.

Prince Avalask began to feel a desperate impatience overcoming him as Maverick thwarted his every attempt to bring them down.

Savaul and Gataan stayed diligently with Dreya while Prince Avalask was out hunting the Zhauri, but the curse made another attempt on her life when a freak earthquake shook the entire structure of her sturdy hideout and brought the stone roof down on her.

Prince Avalask heard her cry for help within seconds, and from across the continent he was able to leap and vanish her out from beneath the collapsing building before the falling debris crushed her.

"She almost died last night," Prince Avalask snarled as Izfazara and Gramsaf looked to each other in dismay. "I'll attack Hakkrui mentally while Maverick and Iquis are both asleep. I will be in and out without Iquis ever knowing I was there."

"Your intents for harm have woken Maverick from a dead sleep before," Gramsaf warned. "If he senses you and wakes Iquis, that mage will kill you with a thought. You've said it yourself — his mental attacks are exponentially more powerful than yours."

"Yes, but I have a new idea. I will *only* go looking for the curse, and not mean them any harm whatsoever. I'm sure Maverick must be keeping it nearby, and he only wakes up because he can sense my intents are a danger to him. If I'm not a threat, if I'm *only* there to find the curse, I don't think I'll wake him." The family listened with worried skepticism as he assured them, "I will be careful. Maverick won't know I'm there until it's too late to call for Iquis, and Iquis won't know I'm there until I'm gone, curse in hand."

Izfazara was running a hand down his beard in distress. "This may be something we have to allow," he finally conceded, looking to his brother. "A mind attack is a terrible risk, but we also can't afford for our next Epic to be killed before it's born. If Avalask is positive he can get to Maverick without Iquis knowing, I'm willing to consider it.

Surprisingly, Gramsaf was the last holdout, and Prince Avalask nearly found his father's concern touching. Sure, it was Escali survival on his mind rather than any sort of fatherly love preventing his approval, but Prince Avalask had learned to appreciate what he could get.

"I can do this," Prince Avalask assured his father. "Then the curse will be over, and we won't have to worry about whether or not Dreya can survive long enough to have this baby. The Zhauri are probably sleeping right now. I could have this over and be back before morning if I leave quickly."

"My hopes are not high, Avalask," Gramsaf said hesitantly. "But I concede this may be the only chance you have left to save your mate and your heir. I would not deny any man the opportunity to at least try."

Prince Avalask nodded his appreciation, and tried to focus on the positive in his father. For all his cold indifference, this was the one thing that seemed to strike emotion in the man — that he knew the cruel suffering of losing a mate and wished for nobody else to ever experience such agony.

"You must be incredibly vigilant with your own safety," Izfazara told him with a nod. "And promise us you will abandon the endeavor at the first sign of trouble. Our people could never recover from losing you."

"I swear to you both that I will be home by morning," Prince Avalask replied. Gramsaf and Izfazara exchanged one last look of concern before they both nodded their permission for him to leave, and he leapt quickly away before they could have a chance to doubt themselves.

He reappeared near the last place he'd seen the Zhauri — a moonlit camp in the glacial north, just behind a jutting cliff that had blocked them from the freezing winds coming down from the mountain tops. Prince Avalask was hit with a blast of the northern gusts and felt the sting of tiny ice shards scratching his face as he threw up a hand to block the next howling squall.

He stepped closer to examine the camp they'd abandoned and found their fire had gone completely cold — meaning they'd probably been gone at least a day.

He couldn't use magic to track them with Zeen keeping the

group shaded, but he could follow their scent like any Escali. Normally the blustery, icy weather would have been a hinderance, but the Zhauri kept five male dogs with them who quite liked to mark everywhere they went. An Escali toddler would have been able to track them.

It was the middle of the night, and Prince Avalask focused on one thing as he followed their scent through the rocky terrain, where snow only ever momentarily dusted the cliffs before being blown away again.

I mean no harm.

I'm not coming to attack.

I only want to destroy the curse.

If he could honestly convince himself he wasn't following the Zhauri to attack them or cause any harm, that was his best chance of not waking Maverick. But he had to mean it.

Prince Avalask finally came to the outskirts of their new camp and he looked ahead with the most benevolent thoughts he could muster. He almost cheered when he found Maverick soundly asleep in a tent by himself, having no awareness of Prince Avalask's approach. Hakkrui kept watch from among the trees and the other three members of the Zhauri Brotherhood slept in a tent beside Maverick's.

Prince Avalask turned invisible and crept closer as he promised himself he wouldn't hurt them no matter what. He was here for the curse only.

He hunkered into a tiny hollow beneath several bushy ferns where his body couldn't be found once he was fully immersed in the mental endeavor, and he checked again to see that he hadn't woken Maverick. Everybody was sleeping soundly except Hakkrui.

Prince Avalask reached with his mind and took control of Hakkrui, facing barely any resistance as he locked the Zhauri's suddenly panicking consciousness into a back corner of his own mind.

Prince Avalask was entirely in Hakkrui's body now, with no Epic powers left to sense if he'd woken Maverick or anyone else. All he had were Hakkrui's eyes to see through, and he wriggled the Zhauri's fingers in front of his face like they were his own.

Hakkrui's consciousness screamed from the depths of his mind, and Prince Avalask just gave him a gentle shushing in return. *I'm not here to hurt anyone,* he thought to the trapped man.

Benign thoughts. There was no reason to consider him a threat.

Prince Avalask took a step forward, and spotted a bat flying overhead, which he brought to an abrupt stop in mid-air with barely a twitch of his fingers. Hakkrui's powers were utterly effortless. Prince Avalask knew how to stop motion with his own magic, but it wasn't nearly as powerful as what this Zhauri had to work with.

He prowled into the Zhauri camp, and none of the furry dogs beside the fire gave him more than a second glance. He picked up a lantern and walked straight to Maverick's tent and stepped inside.

Maverick was already on his feet with a sword in his hand when Prince Avalask stepped inside as Hakkrui, and the Zhauri's leader looked him over for only a moment before understanding crossed his face. He folded his arms and broke into a low laugh. "Oh, Avalask. How clever of you," he said, cupping his chin in disbelief. "*Clever*, but so unwise."

Prince Avalask felt a sudden dread that Maverick may have already woken Iquis, but he had to believe Iquis was still asleep. It killed him that he had no powers to just check.

He should leave. This was the first sign of trouble, and he'd promised he would leave. But he couldn't.

"I don't think it so unwise myself," Prince Avalask said,

stepping forward to hold a hand out and freeze any motion Maverick might think to perform. "I could kill you here and now. It would be easy."

He had to allow slight motion again for Maverick to give him any reply, and Maverick merely broke into a grin in return. "Killing me doesn't break the curse."

"No, but I suppose I could allow you to live, in exchange for telling me where to find it."

Maverick chuckled casually to himself again — a sound that absolutely infuriated the Epic.

He held the life of Prince Avalask's wife and unborn baby in his hands, and he had the audacity to laugh in his face. Prince Avalask had never wanted to rip his throat out with his teeth so badly in his life.

"You are in a bigger bind than I am here, Avalask," Maverick said with a confidence that rattled him. This was what they did though — they exuded confidence in every defeat to make their opponent give up. Prince Avalask was certainly not at the disadvantage here. "You only have as long as Iquis is asleep. The moment he wakes up and comes over here to investigate, you're as good as dead."

"Sounds like we have all night then," Prince Avalask said, his voice sounding especially threatening from Hakkrui's mouth.

"Ah yes. All night for what? You can threaten all you want, but we both know you don't have what it takes to get the curse's location from me."

"How much would you like to wager on that?" Prince Avalask asked, stepping closer as he pulled two of Hakkrui's hidden daggers out from his sleeves.

"Pain is nothing to me," Maverick hissed in return as Prince Avalask stepped up and contemplated where to cut first. Where would hurt the most without being fatal? "And this is *why* you had

167

no right to take that baby from me," Maverick added hatefully. "You've never been better than me. Everything I would have taught that kid, they just learned from you instead."

Those were the words that made him stop. He knew Maverick was saying them in an attempt to prevent Prince Avalask torturing him, but… Prince Avalask *was* better. He was better than this. Better than the Zhauri. It was the only reason he deserved to fight, because he consistently chose to be better.

And instead of cutting into the man, Prince Avalask took another step forward and searched him.

And that was when a different hint of fear crossed the Zhauri's face.

"You think I keep the curse with me?" Maverick hissed. "You're a fool, Avalask. It's nowhere near—"

Prince Avalask froze the man's jaw with a twitch of Hakkrui's fingers and said, "You'll forgive me if I don't take your word for it."

The grey clothes had pockets *everywhere*, and Prince Avalask was positive he didn't find all of them. But he did find a map, a letter, a tiny notebook, and a key around Maverick's neck before he stepped back to search the rest of tent.

Finally convinced the curse wasn't in the tent, Prince Avalask leaned to examine the spoils he'd gathered.

Maverick finally looked worried, and he began to thrash and struggle against the unmovable hold of Hakkrui's magic.

"Is this… Glidria's handwriting?" Prince Avalask asked, holding the letter up as Maverick's face reddened in anger. "I'm not sure whether I'm more inclined to read it or rip it into tiny bits…"

Maverick's eyes went wide, and Prince Avalask said, "Tell me where that curse is hidden, and we can part in peace, Maverick. You'll never have to see me again."

Prince Avalask flicked the map open and added casually, "I'll give you a moment to decide."

He glanced over the map's details to see every city marked with multiple numbers and labels. They said things like:

Keldrosa:
Leader — 25
Population — 50,000
Defense — 1350
Intelligence — 1125
Value — 525

And Prince Avalask's brows pulled into a deep frown as he tried to fathom why Maverick was putting such values on each of the Human cities. Was he planning to *conquer* them?

He looked back up to see Maverick's nostrils flared and a hateful glower in his eyes, but he couldn't possibly hate the Epic more than Prince Avalask loathed him in return.

The danger that Prince Avalask and Fallistra had both sensed in this man was clearly grounded in some sort of reality if these numbers on the map were any indication. Prince Avalask couldn't even imagine a scenario where placing values like these on each city could end in something *good*.

He held up the notebook and then Glidria's letter, weighing which he should peruse first.

Definitely the notebook. Then if Maverick still wasn't talking, he was going to hold Glidria's letter to the nearest candle and burn it.

Prince Avalask wasn't so perfect that he wasn't vindictive.

"How embarrassing it must be to have another man going through your diary," Prince Avalask mused as he flipped through the first few pages. He could see Maverick struggling his hardest now as Prince Avalask saw how he liked to sketch and put his ideas onto paper in organized lists and columns. "You even write about your dreams?" Prince Avalask simpered, wanting to gag as he saw the next few pages held sketches of his sister's face from years long past. "And is this... Aw, Maverick, baby names? Who thought a man such as yourself could be so tender?"

Prince Avalask felt a cruel smile coming to his face as he began to feel better and better about this. This was more devastating than sticking knives into flesh — he was airing out his heart's deepest held secrets where he was able to openly mock them and keep digging. He'd never hated anyone the way he hated Maverick, and a part of him reveled in the sight of the Human's face turning purple in his futile struggle.

Prince Avalask saw a new sense of desperation as he flipped over the next heart-filled pages and Maverick finally began to make desperate noises to get his attention.

"What's wrong? Am I getting to the good parts?" Prince Avalask asked, holding the tiny notebook up as he flipped another page, deliberately slow and studious as he examined more lists of cities and values assigned to them. Maverick was trying to shake his head to tell him something, and Prince Avalask met his eyes with a sneer. "I'll let you speak, but first you have to promise not to scream the moment I release your jaw."

Maverick shot him a disgusted, indignant sneer, as though to snarl, *The leader of the Zhauri Brotherhood does not scream for help.*

Prince Avalask allowed just enough movement for Maverick to move his jaw, and stepped inconsiderately close to hiss, "Tell me where that curse—"

Maverick took an unexpected breath and quickly bellowed, "IQUIS!"

Prince Avalask froze the word before Maverick could even finish it, but he could hear movement in the next tent over, and cursed that all his Epic senses were back in his real body. He had to abandon his hold on Hakkrui before Iquis arrived, and he didn't

170

have any way to tell if that would be in the next few seconds or not.

And the moment he relinquished control of Hakkrui's body, he'd be leaving behind all the findings from Maverick's person. He dropped the notebook and flicked open Glidria's envelope to read her first few lines from the full page.

Maverick,

I love your ideas for all that our baby could be. They are especially grand and mildly frightening, but that's what I love most about you. Your thoughts are never shy or meek, and if our child inherits your ambition and my status and good looks, I really think this world will be theirs for the taking. I fully believe you could improve your position to the point...

Prince Avalask cursed that he heard footsteps approaching the tent, and he leapt back into his own body before the letter said anything of real consequence. All it proved was that he'd been right to not give Archie to his father, who clearly wanted to use him for something along the lines of world domination.

He returned to his own body and flexed his fingers as he looked back to the commotion in the Zhauri camp. Hakkrui was apologizing profusely as he handed back all the items he'd taken off Maverick, and Maverick stormed out of his tent to shout, "That was a mistake, Avalask, one you'll pay for in ways you can't yet imagine!"

Avalask, where in shanking life are you?! a more desperate voice cried into his mind. *You have to come home! We need you!*

It was Savaul, and he could feel in the tone that something was wrong, and that he'd been trying for a while to get through to Prince Avalask while he was controlling Hakkrui.

"Search the trees!" Maverick called to the others as Iquis came unnervingly close to Prince Avalask's position and he disappeared.

171

Prince Avalask landed in the Obsidian Tower beside Savaul, who had panic written across his face. "Get over here! It's Dreya!" he said, grabbing Prince Avalask's arm to steer him into the nearest room as his whole body grew cold in terror.

Dreya was surrounded by their best healers. A whole tray of bloody rags sat beside her, and tears streaked her face.

"No," he breathed, rushing to her side as he felt for the life inside her. It was recovering from a great scare, but was still strong and growing. "Ok, the baby's alright—"

"Yeah, no thanks to you!" she shouted, shoving him back. "Everyone else, get out!"

He froze with a new kind of fear as everyone else stood and retreated from the room. He'd never seen her cry, and she'd never been angry with *him.*

"You," she said, pointing furiously as she broke into more tears. "What are you *doing?*"

"I'm so sorry. I didn't know anything had happened. I was almost onto something, and I thought—"

"You know what *I thought,* Prince Avalask?" she retorted. "I thought you would be here if there was a problem. Instead, I almost lost the baby tonight because you were *so busy,* out settling your blood feud with Maverick!"

He gaped at her for a moment, and she said, "I *thought* I would get to spend my last months *with* you, but I haven't seen you in weeks," she said, dissolving into more tears. He tried to move closer to comfort her, but she shoved him back again. "You've abandoned everything you care about in this obsessive hunt for him, and it has to stop!"

"Dreya," he said softly, "I've only been after Maverick because he has the curse—"

He stopped himself, because his trip to the Zhauri camp had been more than that. He'd been reveling in the suffering he finally

172

got to inflict on his greatest enemy. He'd been there for more than just the curse — he was there to satisfy his own vendetta too.

"And I'm asking you to stop," she said as she wiped at her eyes. "We could spend the next few months trying to stave off the inevitable, or we could spend it living." His shoulders sank as she said, "I want to go out to the cities with you again and help people. I envisioned us spending our evenings together, reading about… *babies*, and getting ready to keep us both alive when it comes time for it to be born."

She was asking him to *give up*, to accept that their fate was inevitable.

"Dreya, I can still get that curse," he insisted. "I just need more time."

"That curse is going to ruin all the time we have left. Stop obsessing over it, Avalask. You tried to get it, and nothing you tried worked. Now I'm asking you to be here for me."

He watched her for a long moment, feeling miserable. How could he give up? How was he supposed to live through this, knowing he might have been able to change the outcome?

"Alright," he said softly.

"Alright?" she repeated. "As in, you're going to stop hunting for Maverick, and be present?"

He nodded and said, "I'm sorry I wasn't here."

She finally set a hand in his and gave him a weak, pitiful smile. "I've missed you."

He reached to hug her and felt the familiar calmness that only she could give him. "I do have one bit of good news, if it might help you to forgive me."

"What is it?"

He gave her a quick squeeze and said, "We are definitely having a boy."

Dreya lurched back, and looked at his face in disbelief, as though

173

she was afraid to get her hopes up. "You're *sure*?"

"Very sure. I had to look to make sure he was safe, and well… it's hard to miss."

"Oh thank life," she breathed a huge breath of relief as she set a hand across her stomach. "I can't believe it. I was so worried."

Prince Avalask frowned and said, "Weren't you the one who was positive it would be a boy to begin with?"

"As if I had any control over it," she retorted as she wiped beneath her eyes to dry them. "I just didn't want you to have another thing to worry about. But if it's a boy…"

"The curse won't touch him," Prince Avalask finished her thought.

The only one it would actively be after was Dreya.

It wasn't a solution, but it was something.

Prince Avalask

Chapter Seventeen

And so Prince Avalask and Dreya lived.

Not happily ever after, but the fullest, most joy-inspired lives they could find. They helped everyone they could help. Prince Avalask finally agreed to spar with his champion of a wife, even though she ran out of breath in the first minute and he fought purely defensively to avoid striking her. It wasn't quite the match Dreya wanted, but she relished it anyway.

Every single evening, they found a new corner of the world to watch the daylight fade. They made it a nightly tradition to curl up and watch the sun as it set behind snowcapped mountains, or cast rainbows across raging waterfalls, or threw pink and orange hues into the clouds above green valleys and sparkling rivers.

It felt so good to just *be*.

They visited everyone Dreya had ever known, just to spend time, and learn, and say hello. There were never any goodbyes — they just traveled across the continent and said many, many hellos.

And they prepared.

Prince Avalask had their healers bring him every book they had about childbirth and complications. This was how he would protect her, by reading and reading and reading, and being ready for every single thing that could go wrong. He learned everything he could possibly need to know, including lots of things he certainly never *wanted* to know.

Dreya sat at the nearby desk every evening, and as he read, she would write.

"I want to name him Vack," she said as she held up a blank sheet of paper with just one line at the top.

My Dearest Vack,

Prince Avalask's heart sank as he realized it was a letter, and he asked, "What are you going to write to him?"

"Everything," she replied, turning back to the mostly-blank page. "Every bit of advice I've learned in my life, and every mistake by which I learned it. I'll tell him stories, and wish him a happy day of life in a separate letter each year, and… I'm going to write him a whole stack, to let him know how much I love him, and that there's nothing in the world he could possibly do that would change that. It will never be the same as a mother's hug, but… I want to make these letters feel as close to love as I can. And I want him to know I'll never truly be gone."

Prince Avalask turned his eyes quickly back down to the book in his hands and blinked rapidly to hide how much that pained him.

"I'll leave one for you too," she said softly. "So you know I'm still with you when the pain feels like it's too much."

"Dreya, I can't read like this," he said as his eyes blurred with tears.

"Sorry, go back to your reading. I just want to make sure you tell him about this one day. About the hours I spent hunched over this desk with cramping hands and ink all over my fingers."

"It's on your face too," Prince Avalask said, glancing up with amusement to where she kept tapping her inky fingers against her chin in thought, then smearing it as she rubbed at her temples. "It's everywhere."

"Good. I want you to tell him all about it. And there are going to be a couple letters that tell him to come to you for a hug, which is ultimately from me."

"Thanks for the heads up," Prince Avalask replied. "I'll be sure to coat myself in ink first so he can get the full experience."

Dreya snorted a laugh and returned to her writing. "I think that would be fitting."

Dreya did die.

It wasn't in childbirth, like everyone suspected it would be. Prince Avalask made sure of that. She gave birth to a healthy spitfire of a baby boy who would accept nobody's embrace except his mother's. She held Vack every hour from the moment he was born until the very end, which was about a week later.

Everything kept going more and more wrong in the days after the birth — things that no book had ever touched on. And when her condition finally reached the point Prince Avalask couldn't possibly keep her heart beating another moment, his entire world shattered apart.

The days following Dreya's death were filled with nothing more than confusion and pain.

Prince Avalask curled in on himself and couldn't breathe. He couldn't take care of little baby Vack. He fell into the Escali's coping mechanism of *norithe*, where his higher thoughts completely shut down, and he existed in a state of nothing more than emotion — allowing him to feel his devastation thoughtlessly, until the pain reached a point where it could be managed again.

He would question for the rest of his life if it had really happened, but as he saw it, he was certain the apparition he saw of

Sir Avery was true and real. The Human Epic walked straight up to him, where Prince Avalask lay crippled by grief — an easy, helpless target. Sir Avery had looked him over with what looked to be pity, and calmly told his counterpart, "You have ten days."

Gramsaf approached him some time after that and shook him roughly by the shoulders. "Avalask!" he shouted, but Prince Avalask could hardly respond. "Avalask, you have to get somewhere safe."

Prince Avalask just pulled his arms over his head and blocked the noise until he felt his father shaking him more forcefully.

"I know this grief you feel," his father growled through the haze. "I'm not asking you to snap out of it. We will hold them off until you've recovered, but you have to recover somewhere else!"

His father hauled him to his feet, and Prince Avalask could just barely feel through the fog of nothing that there was real panic emanating from Gramsaf. There were real attackers inside their residence, but he wasn't asking Prince Avalask to fight them. For once in his life, Gramsaf was only trying to protect him. "Go!"

Prince Avalask leapt and reappeared in the least likely place the Humans would ever look for him — it was a horse ranch up in the north, owned by two women he trusted with his life.

Sass and Flora were both in the main living area, sitting to eat their dinner as they laughed at an old shared story. Prince Avalask didn't announce himself, greet anyone, or even come through the front door. He landed in the closest room that smelled of Humans, crawled onto the large bed in front of him, and blacked back out into the fog of nothing.

They'd find him in their own time.

Prince Avalask was only vaguely aware of the moment Sass and Flora found him and their initial panic as they tried to figure out

178

what to do. They eventually realized there was nothing, and they simply kept watch over him as he slept in an unthinking daze.

Dreya was gone, and the part of him that craved her company, and panicked when he thought she was in trouble, and felt an attachment to her, so real, it felt like half of his body had been ripped away — that part of him had been decimated. Half his heart was gone, and could never be replaced.

Every time he would gain enough coherence to even remember why he was in pain, he would fall back into the cycle of devastation.

Gone.

Dead.

He could never feel the calm she could bring him, never smell her sweet scent, never kiss her inky face, or smile at the way she improved those around her and encouraged them to be better.

Prince Avalask didn't even know if he would ever be able to look at Vack without breaking down. All this so they could have their little boy. Vack would be half *her*, he'd grow to look like her, maybe even act similar, and Prince Avalask was in danger of being the worst father in the world when he wasn't sure he could bear to look at that baby.

Prince Avalask didn't know how long he'd lay curled in despair, but he finally pried himself out of the unfamiliar bed when his parched throat couldn't go another hour without water.

He trudged into the next room, and Sass and Flora both leapt from their chairs when they saw his half-dead face peek out from the bedroom.

"Prince Avalask, come in here! You've been asleep over a *week*," Flora fussed as she hustled to the other side of their river-rock fireplace to grab water from the table. "You must be so hungry, and thirsty. Come in. We'll take care of you."

He gave them a meager nod of thanks as Sass moved to grab him and make sure he made it to the table without collapsing. "You had

179

best know how much we love you," she told him as she helped him sit and Flora pushed a glass of water in front of him. "We've been sleeping on the floor for the past week. My back is too old for this, Prince Avalask. We Humans are fragile."

"Sassilda, let the man drink some water!" Flora scolded as Sass threw her hands up in bafflement.

"I'm not stopping him!"

"It's been a week?" Prince Avalask repeated numbly.

"You can stay here as long as you need," Flora told him kindly. "I think sleeping on the floor has reminded us to be thankful for all we have."

Prince Avalask looked to Sass, who gave a dramatic shrug and said, "Will you drink your water already? I'm clearly not allowed to say anything until you do."

He gave a weak smile and took the glass for a sip, realizing as soon as it touched his lips how incredibly thirsty he was. He drained the whole thing, and as soon as he set the glass down, Sass looked to Flora and demanded, "Now can I ask what happened?"

"We can guess, Sassilda," Flora retorted as Prince Avalask turned his eyes to the table and considered going back to sleep again.

"It was your wife, wasn't it?" Sass asked.

He nodded and they each reached out a hand to set on his.

"It wasn't... the baby too, was it?" Flora asked anxiously.

He shook his head and muttered, "No, baby's fine."

"Was it a boy?" Sass asked, and he nodded again. She and Flora exchanged a look of at least mild relief. They knew of the curse. They knew just about everything. He hadn't erased a single story from their minds before letting them leave the Translation Program. Darin, yes. But not Sass and Flora.

Prince Avalask glanced out to the world to see what was happening. Savaul, Gataan, Gramsaf, and Izfazara were all deep in

180

discussion, hidden away in Tethi Rakna — the one place they were safe while Prince Avalask was indisposed. And Sir Avery was at the walls of Treldinsae, tearing them down *again*.

Which meant ten days had already passed. His time to mourn was over, but he couldn't muster the energy or the will to go out and fight Sir Avery. He could barely muster the strength to walk.

"Let's get you something to eat," Flora said, giving his hand a squeeze before she stood to retreat to their little kitchen area. "How does a nice warm soup sound?"

"Fine. Thank you," he mumbled as he folded his hands on the table and lay his forehead down on them. As Flora busied herself, he spoke straight into the table, "Avery's already out attacking our cities again."

He could feel Sass's dismay, although his eyes remained closed and his head lowered. "You haven't been here ten days yet," she replied.

"I didn't come straight here. I don't know how long I was mourning before we were attacked."

"You think the enemy was trying to kill you while they knew you were indisposed?"

"Probably. Not Avery, but the rest of them would know I was helpless."

He heard Sass's hiss of disapproval, but he still left his head down.

"What are you going to do, Prince Avalask? Sit here and eat soup while Sir Avery kills people you care about?"

"I guess so," he replied, sinking even further into the table in his misery as a thought of Dreya flitted through his mind again. He still had her letter. He hadn't been able to open it.

"You know…" Sass said thoughtfully. "You live your whole life taking care of others. I think that for this chapter in life, it's alright to take a moment to take care of you."

181

He released a deep sigh of disappointment that *that* was the best wisdom she had to give. "What are you saying, Sass?" he muttered.

"You *do* need to pick your forehead up off the table, but Prince Avalask, take another day to recover. Instead of going out to fight Sir Avery, you could go see that little boy of yours. Bring him back here, and let him remind you of how to live."

Prince Avalask gritted his teeth and took an ugly, sniffling breath before he said, "I can't even look at him, Sass. All he'll ever do is remind me of Dreya."

"That... makes sense," Sass said, moving into the chair next to his to rest her arms on the table beside him. "But instead of letting it break you, you should try to let it warm you. That little baby is half you and half Dreya. Can you think of anything more beautiful?"

Prince Avalask dissolved back into tears again, because *no*, there was not anything more beautiful.

"Go visit him. He may be able to help you."

Prince Avalask nodded, and the mild fear crossed his mind that his family would know he was coherent if he went to get the baby. They'd all be outraged to know he could be helping and wasn't. But Sass was right — he did deserve to recover for a short spell. If he went running into battle right now, there was a very real chance he would be destroyed.

He lifted his head and looked to Sass beside him, and she set a hand on the side of his face.

Sass looked straight into his eyes and used her wisest, most serious voice to say, "You. Look. *Terrible.*"

He exhaled a pitiful laugh and replied, "I'll go see him, but you will not be rid of me so easily."

"Bring him back with you," she said with a glance to the kitchen. "Flora will be beside herself — she loves babies. And she's making this soup just for you. You can't disappoint her."

"No, that would be the end of everything," he agreed with feeble humor. Prince Avalask looked out to locate his little Vack, and found the baby safely in the mountain fortress of Tethi Rakna.

He had to appear in the mountain crevices and walk through the icy canyons into Tethi Rakna sine he couldn't leap through the city's jump-shield — but he did so invisibly.

The fresh air was good in his lungs, and walking felt like a foreign skill he was just in the early stages of learning. The walking got easier as he made it into Tethi Rakna, but his fear and uncertainty only grew.

He finally found the stand-in mother Dreya had found for little Vack — her name was Nolra, and he gave her a terrible startle when he became visible in the doorway of her little sitting room.

"Prince Avalask!" she exclaimed, already in a defensive position as though to confront an attacker.

"Sorry," he said softly, giving her a weak smile as she quickly knelt. "You don't have to kneel, Nolra. I imagine it would be taxing if you had to show respect every time you approached Vack to feed him."

"I just laid the two of them down, in the back room," she said. "I can almost guarantee they're playing rather than sleeping though. You want me to show you?"

"No, I'm sure I can figure out which one is mine," he said with another feeble smile. He moved into the back room, and did indeed see two little diapered babies trying to wrestle each other for the upper hand. Escali babies were pretty much born with the ability to tumble and crawl — they didn't have to wait for their motor skills like their Human counterparts.

Vack was the smaller one, also the one who was struggling to get up from where he was pinned, but he squealed at the sight of Prince Avalask and managed to tug himself free.

Vack made an awkward dash of a crawl across the little pen and pulled himself up to his feet to coo happily and reach to be held.

And everything else in the room suddenly seemed to fade as that little boy became the only thing in existence. Prince Avalask moved to pick him up, and he hugged Vack to his chest as an instant relief calmed his crippling devastation. Vack snuggled into his chest, and Prince Avalask was overwhelmed by such a strong sense of love and the instinct to protect his baby, there was suddenly nothing else that mattered.

His little Vack *was* half Dreya.

He was strong, curious, and perfect, and Prince Avalask was never going to let anything happen to him.

A part of him wondered if every new parent felt this sort of reverence when they got to hold their babies, or if it was just because of all he'd lost that the moment was all the sweeter.

It didn't matter one way or the other, but a new sense of guilt crept into his chest as he thought of how he was failing all the other Escalis. There were parents and their new babies in Treldinsae, all in grave danger because he wasn't there to defend them.

He tilted Vack onto his back where he could see the little Escali's face, and Vack yawned widely as he reached to grab Prince Avalask's cloak. "I have to go, Vack," he said, reaching to hold his tiny hand. The baby reached and wrapped all ten fingers around his hand to pull him in closer, and he promptly tried to sink his non-existent teeth in to bite him.

"You are as fierce as your mother promised," Prince Avalask said with a pitiful smile, feeling the despair strike again as Vack growled happily and tried to gum him to death. "I have to leave, but I'll be back. I won't be long."

He tried to set the baby back down, but Vack gripped his hand tightly as Prince Avalask lowered him, and he almost couldn't pull the baby off. He carefully dislodged Vack's grip, which was when the baby released a sharp wail. He stood at the edge of their pen

184

and began to cry and reach for him again.

Prince Avalask felt his heart breaking as Nolra came to the doorway. "I won't be gone long," Prince Avalask insisted as guilt tore at him more than it reasonably should.

"It's alright," she assured him. "He'll be waiting for you when you get back."

Vack wailed louder and reached for him with as much reach as his tiny arms could give him.

"I'll return as soon as I can," he assured his son again, the feeling of being a terrible parent already weighing on him.

"Don't feel guilty," Nolra told him with a hint of a smile as she moved to pick up the crying infant. "This just means he loves you."

Prince Avalask just about choked on that sentiment before he turned and fled the room.

He had his own quarters here in Tethi Rakna, and he locked himself in before sitting on his bed to pull out the letter Dreya had given him. Just the sight of it broke him again as all the same thoughts came back to dampen the very life in his soul.

He'd never see her again.

Never hold her.

Every milestone in Vack's life was going to be experienced without her, and Vack was going to live his whole existence without a mother. And the real tragedy was that she would have been *so good* at it.

Prince Avalask held the letter up and looked at his name across the front in her handwriting. He grabbed a larger sheet of parchment and folded it into a new, larger envelope. And across the front of the new one, he wrote:

Only when you're ready to remember.

"I'm sorry," he whispered as he slid Dreya's letter in and used a simple bit of magic to seal the flaps.

He'd known all along he wouldn't be able to live through losing her, but now that it had really happened, he couldn't afford to *not* recover. There were people depending on him. If he couldn't collect himself enough to get out to Treldinsae, the deaths of every Escali in the city would be his fault.

There was really only one thing to do.

He thought through what he was about to do in despair, knowing how much agony it would cause him. But afterward, it wouldn't hurt so bad. He'd be able to pull himself together and be the Epic the world needed.

He was going to make himself forget her.

Prince Avalask charged into the Treldinsae battle just as the Escalis were looking particularly defeated, and cheers echoed through the whole city as he summoned lightning strikes into the ranks of invaders. He took Sir Avery by surprise and blasted the Human Epic right out of the sky.

The Escalis gained their morale back in seconds and pushed their charge against the seemingly unstoppable Human mages. With Prince Avalask at the front of the battle, they were able to repel the invaders, and by the end of the night, he'd helped them rebuild the shattered sections of wall that had come tumbling down.

The moment the battle was decisively over and all injured Escalis had been retrieved from beneath the remnants of their crumbled buildings, Prince Avalask was back in Tethi Rakna to get his son.

Vack was just about beside himself with joy when Prince Avalask came back to pick him up, and Prince Avalask couldn't help a giant grin as he tossed the baby up and caught him again.

"Come on. Let's go see the world."

Vack watched everything around them with fascination as Prince Avalask carried him out of the mountain fortress and showed him the icy cliffs outside Tethi Rakna, sparkling in the moonlight.

He remembered enough of Dreya to know how greatly he'd loved her. He remembered meeting her, and just a few flashes from bonding and from their evenings spent reading and writing, with ink smeared across her face in multiple places. He remembered enough of her to know she was irreplaceable, and to know how much she'd loved him and Vack.

He also knew that losing her had ruined him. If there ever came a day when the world was peaceful enough that he could take some time to himself, he'd open her letter. He'd woven his own memories in and sealed them into the envelope as well, so on the day he finally opened it, he could have his life with her back.

But for now, nothing was more important than the happily babbling baby in his hands. Prince Avalask was going to teach him everything, and raise him to be better than the rest of them. He was going to give Vack the best world he could possibly give him, and tell him every day about how much his mother loved them both.

He leapt to Sass and Flora's northern horse ranch, and Flora almost cried when she got to hold him.

"He's so *mobile*," she exclaimed as he tried to crawl up onto her shoulder. "Prince Avalask, isn't this baby two weeks old?"

"Two weeks plus a few days. You Humans are just about the only creatures in the world who give birth to useless little blobs," he replied with a grin. "The rest of us are born with the ability to get around."

Sass sniggered at the humor as Flora tried to steady the intently listening baby now perched on her shoulder. "You seem a lot... better," she said with an uncertain glance to Prince Avalask.

"Better, yes, but I'm actually famished," he replied with an easy smile. "Nothing a bowl of Flora's glorious soup won't fix."

She and Sass glanced to each other in confusion, and he assured them, "I'm fine. Now can I get some soup or what?"

Vack lunged and wrapped his arms around Flora's face so she couldn't see, and he barked a strange growling resemblance of a giggle as she reached up to dislodge him.

"You know if you ever need to hide him for a little while, you can always bring him here," Sass said as Flora pulled Vack down into her arms and he tried to crawl back to her shoulder again.

"Thanks Sass, but I'm worried the two of you might let him starve. Is it customary for guests here to have to dish themselves up?" He blazed past them into their little kitchen area. He made a dramatic show of opening each cupboard until he found the bowls, and then he scooped one into the soup to fill it.

It felt good to joke and laugh again after the pain and distress of the last few weeks. Of the last several months, really. He finally felt like himself again. He sat in their little dining area and rested his elbow spikes on the table as he looked over the tiny little spoon they used to eat their soup. It was considered poor manners to drink soup straight from the bowl, one of the Human's *many* strange rules when it came to consuming food.

"Excuse me," Sass said, grabbing his wrist to pull his arm up. "Do you mind *not* digging your elbow *death-spikes* into my nice table?"

"Sorry," he said in good humor as he tried to take a bite using the spoon. It was excruciatingly slow to eat like this, and he abandoned the spoon to drink from the bowl like any reasonable person should.

Prince Avalask took Vack to several places across the continent, and landed in Dekaron to show him the way the moonlight glinted off the Obsidian Tower. He leapt into the Epics Hall and walked down its vast length as he waved a hand to light each of the torches.

Vack squealed and reached toward a torch, wanting his father to take it down and hand it to him. "I think we'll hold off on playing with fire for a year or two," Prince Avalask said, shifting Vack up to his shoulder, where he clung tightly and dangled off his back. "You'll sit in here one day too," Prince Avalask said, gesturing to the throne-like golden seat at the end of the hall. "People will come here to ask your help, and you and I will help them. I'll teach you everything I know, and you'll change the whole world."

Vack growled and tried to bite into his shoulder, still not having any teeth to do much at all.

Prince Avalask grabbed Vack and held him up as he plopped into the giant seat and draped his legs over the arm to lean back against the other arm. "Hopefully we'll make this chair a bit more comfortable by the time you're ready to sit in it."

Vack squirmed and giggled as Prince Avalask held him up in the air and just enjoyed the baby's thoughts. Vack had nothing but love in his heart. He was thrilled with the sights of the world around him, and was so happy to be with his father — who smelled more right to him than anyone else.

Prince Avalask smiled and played with him for a little while before he sensed somebody outside the massive doors, hesitating fearfully instead of just knocking.

And Prince Avalask froze for a moment as he looked through the door to see the short golden hair on Archie's head — the same color as Glidria's and Fallistra's. Prince Avalask took a deep breath and decided to think through this logically. He wanted to be angry with Archie for all the devastation his father had caused, but it wasn't Archie's fault — not in the least.

It wasn't his fault he looked so much like Maverick. It wasn't his fault that Glidria had to go and have relations with one of the most dangerous Humans around. He was a good kid.

Prince Avalask spared him the indecision and waved a hand to open the doors. "You can come in," he called as Vack barked a happy greeting down the hall too.

Archie looked like he wanted to crawl away and hide as he made the long trek down the pillar-lined walkway, guilt and misery clear on his face. Prince Avalask was still sprawled on the chair as Archie stopped and knelt for him, and the Epic finally sat up in concern.

"What is wrong with you?" Prince Avalask asked as Archie swallowed hard. "Family doesn't kneel, Archie. Stand back up."

"It's a gesture of respect," Archie said as he stood slowly back up, arms wrapped tightly around his middle, "and... I don't know how else to ever tell you how sorry I am."

Prince Avalask frowned and said, "You don't have anything to be sorry about."

"Savaul told me what happened. He said that you begged Maverick to destroy the curse. That you offered to give him anything in the world, but he wanted to make you suffer."

"Yeah, I hope you don't mind, Archie, but I am going to kill your father one day."

Archie nodded to say that was fine with him, then added softly, "I just want you to know how sorry I am. I'm sorry I look like him, and I'm sorry this is happening..."

Prince Avalask let a sigh escape and reminded himself to have a talk with Savaul after this.

Savaul took every possible chance he could to torment Archie. It was everything from outright attacks and ambushes to small jabs — calling him Archibald, telling him how much he looked like his father, and hinting that Fallistra and Glidria would both be alive if not for his abominable existence.

"None of this is your fault, no matter what Savaul tries to tell

190

you," Prince Avalask said. "You shouldn't be talking to him."

"Everything feels like my fault," Archie said uncomfortably. "Maverick would have broken the curse if Fallistra hadn't chosen to steal me away and raise me alone. She'd still be alive. Mother might not have died having me. Dreya would still be alive..."

Prince Avalask swallowed at the name and felt a jolt of pain, but it was a pain he could handle.

"And I just want you to know I'm going to break it. The curse," Archie said. "I'll find a way, so that Vack can love someday without fear. Maybe you and I can love again too..."

"Don't you ever go near your father, Archie," Prince Avalask said with the most serious voice he could wield. "I've lost too much to see you fall into his hands now."

Archie threaded his fingers absentmindedly into his hair and tugged at it as he turned his eyes to the floor and muttered, "You said I'm not like him."

"You're not, but you also don't know him. He will change you. He is stronger than you could ever hope to resist."

"I believe you, but I just..." Archie hesitated. "I need to make up for all the pain and destruction I've caused. I don't ever want you to regret that you helped Fallistra save me."

Prince Avalask realized he would need to do something to ensure Archie didn't go to Maverick looking for the curse. He'd lie and say Maverick didn't have it any more. He'd somehow have to convince Archie there was absolutely nothing to be gained by approaching the man, because this poor boy could not fathom who he was dealing with.

"Archie, I will never regret that I helped her save you. It doesn't matter who your father is — you're part of our family. And we don't all have to become our fathers." He held Vack up, determined to never treat his own son the way Gramsaf had treated his children. "Your choices are what matter. You just have to consistently *choose* not to be him."

Archie nodded and watched Vack for a moment as the baby cooed and reached for Archie to come play. "I hope Vack grows to be like you," Archie said softly.

"So do I, but better," Prince Avalask said, looking to his happy little baby who didn't know a thing about the world he'd been born into, or how greatly he might affect it. "I'm still a bit new to this, but I really think it's every parent's vision for their children to surpass them. We teach and guide them in the hopes they'll be better than us."

Archie nodded and Prince Avalask finally looked to him. "You're one of ours, Archie, but I still need you to promise me you will never go near your father."

Archie nodded solemnly and met his gaze.

"I promise."

Prince Avalask

Epilogue

Prince Avalask had loved Dreya with his entire soul, but his love for Vack was something even more indescribable.

That boy had been an absolute spitfire from the day he entered the world, and time seemed to evaporate as he grew.

A year after he was born, Prince Avalask found himself running to a family meeting with the toddler in hand, exclaiming, "He just lit his bedding on fire. Vack, do it again! Show them!" Everybody in the family had gathered around as they handed their little black haired, green eyed Epic a piece of parchment. Vack growled, then sputtered, and then lit the page on fire, squealing in delight at the sight of the flames.

The whole family loved watching him grow, especially as he began to talk and say things like *I love you.* As adorable as he was, Prince Avalask also suddenly found himself bombarded by thousands of questions about powers, Epics, Humans, Escalis, and how *literally everything* in the world worked. Prince Avalask had to teach him to play with Mir and his other friends without hurting them, and constantly kept him in gloves to prevent accidental burns or lightning bolts.

At three years old, Vack snuck out of the Obsidian Tower — the first time he'd ever left. Prince Avalask nearly had a heart attack when he realized his whole world was gone, but he quickly located

Vack outside. His rascal of a son had gone and found himself a cute little *girl*, and the next week was full of absolute refusal to do anything at all unless she was allowed to come over and play.

Four years old brought about quite a bit more magical control. Vack lived for their daily training sessions as Prince Avalask invented new games to practice their powers. They would see who could levitate rocks through hoops more accurately. They'd compete to see who could burn a tree to ashes faster. And Prince Avalask adopted Dreya's approach, to never let him win. If Vack was going to beat his father in something, he was going to earn it.

Prince Avalask still had to battle Sir Avery, and defend their cities, and help the sick, and gather information, and consult with Escali leadership, but he did everything in his power to make sure he spent time training his son every single day.

Vack was five and just starting to learn about jumping when Prince Avalask froze in the middle of training him to land gracefully. Watching Vack land in a heap every time was amusing, but not exactly helpful.

"Da? What's going on?" Vack asked, tilting his head in curiosity. He reached toward his father's face on impulse, which was the way they usually exchanged thoughts and ideas, but Prince Avalask blocked Vack's inquiring thoughts from seeing what he could see.

Savaul and Gataan had a small, blonde Human girl in their hands, and they were running.

From what? To where?

Prince Avalask didn't wonder long. The girl barely looked older than Vack, but due to the excruciatingly slow Human aging process, she was the perfect age, and he knew exactly who she was. "They found her, Vack," he said quickly. "I have to go."

"What?" Vack exclaimed in alarm. "We're not even done with our training—"

Prince Avalask didn't have time to explain further — he'd

196

warned Vack this was going to happen one day, and reached a hand out to vanish his son to a safe, underground hideout with no entrances or exits.

He leapt and reappeared right in front of Savaul and Gataan and snarled, "What are the two of you doing?"

They dropped the terrified little girl, and she crawled away to cower at the base of an aged tree as Savaul spat back, "We found her and we're taking her to Dekaron. Gramsaf wanted her brought straight to him—"

"Our father is *never* going anywhere near that girl," Prince Avalask snapped. Fury welled inside him at the very idea of Gramsaf approaching her.

The tiny Human girl in a dreadfully painted tunic looked up from beneath her protective arm, and Prince Avalask hesitated for a brief moment as he saw the streaks where tears had cut through the dirt on her face.

How could something so meek and frail be the new Human Epic?

Prince Avalask reached to vanish her to the same room where he'd put Vack, and she gasped in horror as she saw the magic in his hands, right before she disappeared.

"I want to know exactly what happened," he demanded, turning back to Savaul. Gataan was clearly just the follower here — the way things always were when he and Savaul got into trouble.

"There's nothing to tell," Savaul spat back. "We found her, now you just came and ruined everything—"

Prince Avalask scanned back through the trees, the way they'd come. He found a dead Human woman and a gravely injured boy, about the same age as the young Epic they'd just taken. And lastly, there was one teenaged Tally girl bent over the dying youngster, her hands soaked in blood as she tried to help him.

"DID YOU JUST KILL THE NEW EPIC'S FAMILY?" Prince Avalask roared, images of his lifelong feud with Avery clouding

his vision in a rage. They may have just carelessly destroyed any hope of the next generation of Epics *ever* getting along.

"I told Gataan not to," Savaul protested. "The boy was still alive—"

"Barely!"

"I can't help how fragile they are," Savaul snarled. "I only meant to knock him unconscious."

Prince Avalask swore and looked back to where several Human mages were about to stumble across the scene, scaring Allie to her feet as she heard them approaching. They would take the boy back to Tabriel Vale and look after him. Prince Avalask would make sure they didn't let him die, and then he was going to be back with a wagonload of questions for the Tally who always had her nose in everything secretive.

"What's her name?" he snapped.

"It's Ebby," Savaul hissed back. "And we're not obligated to tell you everything we do, Avalask. She'll be an incredibly valuable asset to us if we use her right. You need to consider—"

"I'm going to kill you, Savaul," he retorted, looking to the small Epics' room to see Vack hiding in the fireplace as Ebby scrambled back from him in sobbing horror. She'd just caught a glimpse of her lifelong counterpart, and she was having a mental breakdown. "I've got to go, but Savaul..." he stopped and hesitated before he finally asked the question. "Are you *sure* it's the right girl?"

"We're positive," Savaul replied. "She burned me with fire, and she... projects her emotions. You'll feel it. She can make you *feel* her fear. It's unnerving."

"How did you find her?"

"Avery's had her moving between cities, always staying with different powerful families so we'd never spot the pattern again, of where he was showing up to protect her. She doesn't even know she's the Epic. It sounds like she's never met Avery at all."

198

"Alright. I'll be right back. And then I want to hear everything you know about her, and exactly how you found her."

"Remember what she is!" Savaul called after him as Prince Avalask disappeared.

Prince Avalask landed next to the table in the middle of the room as Ebby tucked her head beneath her arms to sob against her legs.

"Don't be afraid of me. I'm all the way over here," he said, trying to soften his voice to sound just a bit less terrifying. The poor girl had her eyes clenched shut and was just barely gasping breaths in her terror, certain she was about to be killed, or eaten alive.

And Savaul was right, she was projecting them — making her terror known as his chest constricted in pain too.

Prince Avalask crept forward and set a hand on her shoulder to numb her emotions, only for a moment. He assured her she was safe, and quickly explained who he was, and gave her the most heartfelt apology he knew how to give as the poor girl hiccupped and wiped at her stinging eyes.

Margaret and Ratuan — those were the names of the two she'd been with. He was just about sick over the fact Savaul and Gataan had harmed them, and wasn't sure he could possibly come up with a punishment severe enough to show them his displeasure. But Ratuan would live. Prince Avalask would stalk in and heal the boy himself if nobody else was getting the job done.

And what in life had Allie been doing there?

Vack had stuffed himself into the fireplace, he was so terrified by the Human girl before them. When he gathered enough courage to dart out and hide behind his father, Prince Avalask couldn't stop himself from wondering what kind of insanity he was suffering to think this might work.

He was going to trap them down here together until they could work out their differences. He was going to make sure they knew one another and had enough time to possibly, *maybe* even become friends, before he sent Ebby back to Humanity.

To say Ebby was horrified when she realized Vack was the new Escali Epic would have been the understatement of the century. And she didn't even *believe* Prince Avalask when he told her she was Sir Avery's daughter. He actually still had a few doubts himself, but he was sure Allie would be able to clear everything up when he tracked her down. That was the very next place he would head after this.

"I know this is hard to hear, especially right now, but this is why you're here," Prince Avalask said in his gentlest voice as the small girl cowered in dread. "I've been looking for you since the day you were born. And I'm..." Prince Avalask hesitated and looked at his hands as though his words had slipped through them. "I'm... sorry to do this to you, but you're going to grow up to be very powerful, Ebby. If you spend the rest of your life battling Vack, like every Human and Escali Epic before you, then it's all a waste."

He didn't want to lay the weight of the entire Human-Escali war onto her shoulders just yet, but she was here for no other reason. The war *had* to end, and Prince Avalask had missed nearly every opportunity he'd ever had to end it.

He'd destroyed his chance to be lifelong allies with Sir Avery. He'd let the opportunity of ruling side by side with Glidria slip through his hands. He'd fallen in love with the vision Dreya had painted for him, of having two sons who would rule the Escalis together, who would have been able to accomplish anything.

A part of him knew he had one last chance to truly impact the future, and it lay with the two kids on either side of him.

Prince Avalask looked into Ebby's sharp Human eyes, so different from his own, but filled with the same light, intelligence, and soul that any Escali might have. Their similarities gave him a hope that leaked into his voice as he said, "If you can somehow manage to get along, the two of you could change everything."

THE END

Pronunciation Guide

However you pronounce these names in your head is perfectly acceptable, but for the sake of resolving those inevitable arguments, here's how I imagine a few of the harder ones.

Avalask – Av-uh-lask

Dekaron – Deck-uh-ron

Dragona – Druh-go-nuh

Driikyn – Dree-ih-kin

Escali – Ess-caw-lee

Escalira – Ess-caw-lir-uh

Gataan – Gat-ay-an

Glidria – Glid-ree-uh

Icilic – Iss-il-ick

Iquis – Ick-wiss

Izfazara – Iz-fuh-zar-uh

Maverick – Mav-rick

Savaul – Suh-vall

Tethi Rakna – Teth-ee Rack-nuh

Zhauri – Zhar-ee

Escali Alphabet

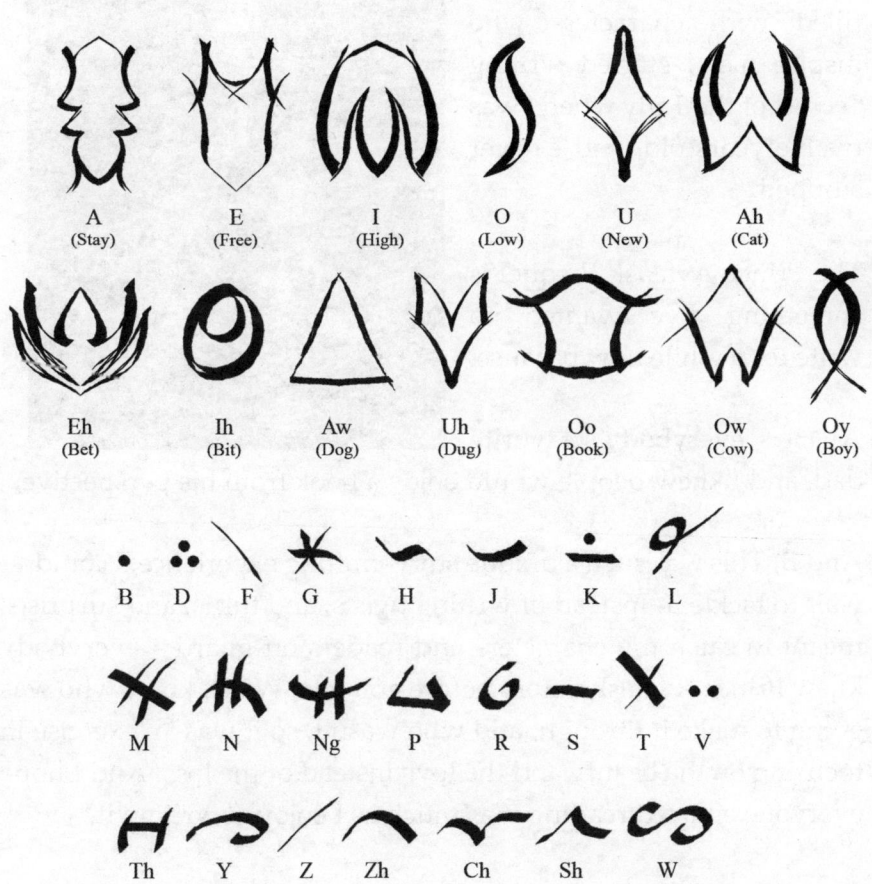

About The Author

My name is Halie, and I love to spend time in magical worlds filled with characters who inspire me. I started writing Secrets of the Tally when I was twelve years old, and I never stopped.

The Prince Avalask Prequel is something I've wanted to write for a while now because:

A) He's everybody's favorite dad, and I knew people would enjoy a book from his perspective.

And B) This was such a unique story-crafting experience, I couldn't wait to tackle it. Instead of writing twists, and turns, and surprises meant to catch my characters and readers off-guard – everybody knew Prince Avalask's story before going in. We all knew who was going to make it through, and who wasn't, so it was an exercise in focusing on the beauty and the love instead of the loss. And I hope everyone enjoyed reading it as much as I enjoyed writing it.

Book Five will be on its way in 2022, and don't miss the children's book starring Macho the puppy – releasing in late 2020.

Stay up to date at www.secretsofthetally.com!